Ambush at
Lakota Crossing

Lakota Crossing was manned by two old codgers and was fifty miles from the nearest town. It had always been the perfect place for an ambush. But when Wayland Lott and his gang of killers planned to rob an army payroll at its way station, they had no idea that one of those men had a bounty hunter on his trail.

Bounty hunting was not the sort of life Jess Logan had expected after the war. He'd had a bit of luck and even earned a reputation, but his luck ran out in Missouri when he ran into the worst blizzard on record. So Logan took on a job at the stage stop at Lakota Crossing to finish out the winter there . . . and when the bandit gang began warring, Jess jumped straight into the action, regardless of the consequences. . . .

Ambush at Lakota Crossing

Terrell L. Bowers

A Black Horse Western

ROBERT HALE · LONDON

ISBN 978-0-7090-9044-1

Robert Hale Limited
Clerkenwell House
Clerkenwell Green
London EC1R 0HT

www.halebooks.com

Typeset by
Derek Doyle & Associates, Shaw Heath
Printed and bound in Great Britain by
CPI Antony Rowe, Chippenham and Eastbourne

CHAPTER ONE

At the end of the war between the Union and the Confederacy, Texas refused to surrender. As a result, an occupation force of northern soldiers took over the state. They instituted military law and crushed any form of rebellion or dissension. There were an untold number of crooked dealings, land grabs and complete repression of the Confederate-supporting population. It was more than many Texans could stand.

After his family ended up homeless and eventually left for New Mexico to start over, Jess Logan took up bounty hunting to keep from starving. He had a bit of luck right away, when he helped capture the Dennison Gang. It was not something he was proud of, as they were all ex-Confederate soldiers, but law had to be restored before Texans could begin to rebuild. With his bounty in hand, he left Texas so he wouldn't have to chase down his own countrymen.

His next prey was Bloody Bill Gates, a ruthless and deadly killer roaming around in New Mexico Territory. The man left a trail of bodies and mayhem to follow. He was cruel and vicious, more beast than man. Jess stayed on his trail into Colorado, where he caught up with him at a small mining town. He was understandably nervous about taking on such a deadly brute, but fate entered into the picture and left a smile on his face. Bloody Bill Gates had ransacked a couple of the miners' shacks and happened to find a jug of homemade applejack.

Jess located him in his camp that night, his horse picketed, a fire burning, with blankets laid out for the night. And there in all of his brutal, menacing glory was Bloody Bill Gates . . . passed out from drinking the wickedly strong liquor. Before he could waken or sober up the next morning, Jess bound him over his horse like a four-point buck, strapped at both his wrists and ankles and cinched tight beneath the animal's belly.

Jess took the man into Denver that way, twelve hours strapped over the back of his horse. Bloody Bill spent the first hour throwing up and another three or four cussing and threatening Jess. However, he was almost too weak to walk by the time Jess dropped him off at the jail.

Even before he could get paid, a traveling news

hound picked up the story, embellished it tenfold, and sold it to several different newspapers throughout the country. Jess hadn't been looking for a reputation, but he had one after that.

Winter set in and times were hard, so Jess kept moving and hunting for men, trying to eke out a living. His next prey was bagged without a whimper. When Jess told him his name the man threw his hands in the air and surrendered.

He turned the man in at a small town and got only a promissory note from the marshal, because they had no bank in town. It was then he learned of a new subject, a nasty man with a gun, named Prince. He had a $200 reward on his head, so Jess set out to find him.

He picked up his trail near the Colorado border and went eastward, following him across Kansas and into Missouri. That's when a major winter storm decided to change the fortune of Jess Logan.

He learned from a barkeep that Prince had learned Jess was on his trail, so finding him was going to be harder than expected. Forewarned, Prince stayed away from most of the larger towns, keeping to the rivers and valleys. Jess stopped to check at outposts, ranches and farms, trying to pick up any information he could. The winter had arrived with the usual number of storms and cold, until mid-December, 1866. Jess was traveling through the

Missouri Valley, along a vast stretch of barren prairie and the range of mountains known as the Patched Skin Buttes. That's when a storm of extraordinary savagery let loose its limitless fury.

Jess arrived at the trading post at Falling Pine Creek and barely managed to put up his horse when the snowfall turned into a roaring blizzard. Alex Kelley, a Dutchman from Pennsylvania, ran the trading post, along with his clerk and long-time friend Louis St Pierre. They were agreeable sorts and invited Jess to stick out the storm.

Day after day, icy cold winds and a ferocious downfall of snow blanketed the mountains. The nearby prairie was windswept by the wicked gusts and gales adding to the snow's three or four feet until the downfall settled and filled the ravines with hundred foot drifts.

On the fourth day of the relentless storm Jess sat down to watch as Dutch and Louis played a game of checkers after breakfast.

'The thermometer was at thirty below at daybreak,' Dutch said. 'Don't remember when it was ever that cold before ... not in a coon's age I'd wager.'

'I feel it,' Louis replied. 'I must have gotten up a dozen times to bank the stove last night. The wind was howling like a crazed banshee and there's no sign of it letting up again today.'

'I'm for thinking I owe you fellows my life,' Jess commented. 'A man out there, caught in this? He couldn't last more than a day or two – probably not more than a few hours without some sort of shelter.'

'Reckon we won't be able to count on having Christmas dinner with the Le Beau boys,' Dutch said. He clarified for Jess, 'They live about fifty miles from here and were going to make a trip to visit for the big day. We was looking forward to the fresh antelope and venison they promised, but ain't no way they will be able to make it here from their trading outfit.'

Louis agreed. 'With this storm, I suspect the three of us will be sitting here by our lonesome come Christmas.'

'If the wind dies down this afternoon, we ought to shovel a pathway to the front door again.'

Dutch's friend smiled at the suggestion. 'You expecting some business later today are you?'

'I doubt anyone will be able to reach us for a week or more, and that's only if this infernal blizzard lets up pretty soon. You know. . . .'

But his words died as the door to the store was suddenly pushed open and three nearly frozen Indians staggered into the room.

'I know them boys!' Louis declared, as they all hurried over to help the trio inside and close the door. 'They are some of Chief Strikes-the-Ree's tribe.' He glanced at Jess and explained, 'The

Hunkpapa Sioux village is located about three miles from the store.'

'Ask what they are doing here,' Dutch said to Louis.

The men were in deplorable condition. Ice caked their clothes, their hands and feet were frozen and all three were so numb from the cold that not one of them could utter a single word.

Dutch and Louis set about thawing them out. It was a tedious process as the body didn't react well to being frozen. When the freeze started to leave the fingers and toes it caused an almost unbearable pain; the hands and feet felt as if someone was pumping each finger or toe full of liquid fire. The internal pressure builds until each of the extremities seemed on the verge of exploding. Being in such dire condition, it took a full half-hour before one of the three Indians was able to speak clearly enough for Louis to understand his words. The weary man relayed an ominous tale indeed.

'The Hunkpapa located their camp down in a coulee, where it was protected from the wind and the elements by an overhanging bluff,' Louis translated for Dutch. 'But the snow got too deep and half the mountain came down in an avalanche early this morning. Their tepees are buried under tons of snow and beyond recovery.' Louis paused while the suffering brave fought to get out the words.

'He says some of their people didn't make it out of the drift and are likely dead. Those who escaped are cold and starving. There hasn't been any food in their camp for two days. A hunting party left to find buffalo several days ago but they haven't returned.'

'Holed up somewhere because of this powerful storm,' Dutch surmised.

Louis asked about the condition and number of survivors. The Indian answered the count was one old man and seventeen women and children. They were exposed to the weather, with no shelter or food and only the clothes on their backs. He feared if they didn't get help soon they would all perish.

Dutch and Louis exchanged a knowing look. 'There ain't no one else to help those people,' Dutch said. 'I reckon they'll all die without help.'

'Might be dead already,' Louis said sadly. 'Only one thing to do.'

'Count me in,' Jess offered. 'I'm a few years younger than you boys and I'm in pretty good physical shape.'

'We're the only chance they have,' Louis said. 'These three braves are too spent from the cold, hunger and exhaustion. They wouldn't make it fifty feet.'

'Let's get a move on,' Dutch agreed. 'Those people don't have much time.'

Gathering felt boots, snow packs, ratskin caps and

fur coats, the trio began to ready themselves for the dangerous trek. Dutch said the survivors would need food if they were to make the trip back to safety. However, there was no way to carry much in the way of supplies, not while fighting the mountain-sized drifts, a razor-sharp wind and a swirling ocean of snow. Dutch looked through the eatables they had received from Yankton on the last delivery – bacon, loaf sugar, coffee and Cayenne pepper. He stuffed the pepper into one coat pocket and they each packed some loaf sugar and strips of bacon in their remaining pockets.

Jess had a heavy coat and a trapper's hat that had flaps which tied under his chin. He put on two pairs of heavy trousers, a double layer of socks and tied the pant cuffs about his boots to keep out the snow. Dutch bundled up and used a woolen scarf around his neck and it covered his face except for his eyes.

The howling wind slammed them full force the instant they stepped outside the door, pelting them with a hail of granules which stung more like grains of sand than snow. From the description given by the Indian, Louis knew the approximate location of the coulee where the Indians had camped. The swirling snow had already covered the tracks of the three Indian braves. Louis knew the campsite was not far from the river so they would try to follow the water-way. It would be a little further to travel, but they couldn't hope to traverse the mighty drifts going cross country and locate the right coulee. Battling the swirling and blowing snow, they proceeded like three blind men, feeling their way with each step.

Louis was half-Indian and Dutch claimed his friend had the instincts of a cross-country guide. He led the way and Dutch and Jess did their best to keep up. When they reached the crown of a small hill, Dutch rose up to walk erect over the crest. A mighty gust blew him right off of his feet. He was tossed like a dry leaf and slammed into a frozen mound of earth. Had he not been wearing so many garments he might have cracked a rib from such an impact.

'Stop fooling about,' Louis yelled to be heard. 'We got to keep moving!'

Dutch swore an oath at the brutal wind and struggled back to his feet. Ducking low, he plunged ahead like a bull going through a thicket of wild rose. Sinking nearly to the waist with each step, it was like trying to climb up the face of a waterfall during flood season.

Louis kept them moving, often forced to crawl on hands and knees, laboriously straining to reach a point where they might glimpse Chief Strikes-the-Ree's village. He told them that the chief had won his name from fighting the Ree people. Their clothing became crusted with ice, their feet and hands grew numb and their faces burned from the constant sting of the frigid wind and blowing snow. Bogged down in one deep snow drift after another, they worked for an hour and managed no more than a few hundred yards. It was exhausting and demoralizing, straining so hard to make so little headway.

But the men were determined and continued the punishing fight, moving with the speed of earth-bound sloths, until Louis finally held up a hand. They had reached the opposite bluffs but they could see nothing but snow. It was like looking over an ocean of white, with undulating waves rising up from stormy waters. The landmarks had been wiped clean, buried beneath the endless sea of wind-formed brows and frozen breakers.

'Damn it all, fellows!' Louis called out over the noise of the whistling wind, 'every gully and hill is buried under the snow. I ain't got the faintest idea where we're at!'

Dutch groaned and Jess let out a woeful sigh. Their desperate battle to save innocent lives and overcome the enormous power of Mother Nature might all be for naught. They were lost. Dutch and Jess crawled up next to Louis. Dutch shouted to be heard. 'What'll we do?'

Louis squinted against the swirling snow. 'If we can get up on that high bluff,' he pointed at a mountain of ice, 'I might be able to get my bearings.'

'We ain't whupped yet,' Dutch vowed. 'Let's have a go!'

The cutting wind ripped and lashed at their bodies making it difficult to move even in a crouch. They had to crawl along on the hazardous crust, inching forward while the driving snow pelted their faces until they could barely see. Louis broke trail and Dutch and Jess stuck to his heels. They continued on their hands and knees, climbing over one bluff and then a second. The precious time being lost ate at their consciences. People could be dying and they were unable to find their way to the campsite. Despair tugged at the hearts of the afflicted trio. What good their sacrifice if they arrived too late to save anyone?

It was then Lady Luck, in a contrary sort of way, decided to lend a helping hand. The edge of the drift they had been crossing suddenly gave way and all three of them plunged down the precipice! They slid and rolled and tumbled, crashing down the mountainside until they landed at the bottom of the cliff, buried in eight feet of snow.

Calling out to one another over the roar of the storm, they dug like moles to regroup and work themselves back up on top of the snow. They emerged to discover they were at the bottom of a ravine.

Louis paused for them to catch their breath and looked skyward toward the peak they had been on. 'That was some ride, huh?'

'Like falling off of the moon,' Dutch replied.

'I've snow down my neck all the way to my long-handles,' Jess bemoaned. 'Think anyone will find us come the spring thaw?'

'They don't turn out young'uns like they used to, Dutch,' Louis said, his frozen face nearly cracking from trying to grin.

'Soft,' Dutch agree, 'this new generation of men are soft.'

Jess uttered a cynical grunt. 'And I thought the odds against me were bad while fighting in the war.' Then he offered up a challenge. 'You boys want to sit here jawing or do we find that Indian camp?'

They picked up their supplies, shook off what snow they could and followed the ravine until they reached the river. For a brief moment the wind let up, possibly to take another deep breath, but the momentary hesitation allowed them to see the other side of the river.

Louis suddenly yelped with joy. 'There!' he shouted, pointing at the opposite creek bank. 'I recognize that scraggly broken tree,'

'Please tell me we're close to the camp,' Dutch called back.

'Come on!' Louis was revitalized. 'We're almost there. It isn't far now!'

CHAPTER TWO

The three men crossed the iced-over river and began to push and plow their way through drifts of snow, working quickly up the nearby coulee. They were winded and their remaining energy almost spent when they burst upon the frozen Indians.

A quick search and they discovered the Indian at the store had been accurate. The tally was one old man and seventeen women and children, alive . . . but all of them were in very poor shape. They had managed to crawl out from the avalanche, carrying with them a few blankets and robes from their crushed tepees. To stave off the bitter cold they had carved out a shallow cave in one of the snow banks and were packed in like so many frogs in a hole during hibernation. There was no fire burning as none of the survivors had the means or dry tinder to start one.

The women had placed the children in the center, trying to keep them as warm as possible. However, they were all near death and only one or two showed an awareness that help – such as it was – had arrived.

'Let's start with that one,' Dutch shouted, indicating a rather sturdy-looking woman. 'She looks more awake than the others.'

Jess and Louis hauled her up by her arms and forced the woman to stand. She resisted their efforts at first, but after some coaxing, she started moving about. When she was revived enough to remain upright on her own they chose a second one and repeated the process. This one was less cooperative and had to be given a firm smack on the cheek to bring her around. Such an uncouth action would have gotten a deadly response from any of the male members of the tribe under ordinary circumstances, but this was life or death.

After the two women were moving under their own power, Dutch cut each a small slice of bacon for them to eat. The effort of chewing took a great deal of prompting as, while their hunger was great, the cold had nearly taken the life out of these women. It was a mighty chore for them to try and grind the frozen bits of meat.

'It's no good,' Louis complained. 'They don't have the strength to eat.'

'I've an idea,' Dutch said. And he laced a piece of

bacon with a healthy dose of Cayenne pepper. Louis told the stronger woman to try it.

She reluctantly inserted the bacon and began the painstaking chore of eating. Her eyes suddenly widened and filled with tears; she began chewing much faster. When she swallowed, she quickly stuffed in a mouthful of snow, but she was now fully awake and ready to help the others.

The burning pepper worked wonders. Dutch gave each frozen woman a few bites of pepper-laced bacon, followed by a chunk of sugar from the loaf. Within a short while all of the adult women had recovered enough to begin working with the children.

The youngsters were equally hard to revive, but once they got a mouthful of pepper, they perked up and were soon able to eat some of the sugar and bacon. It was a painstaking and wearisome job and the continued exertion took a toll on the three men.

Jess had been in the better physical condition, as Dutch and Louis spent most of their time indoors at the trading post. Even so, he suffered from the draining effects of the adruous trek and rousing the women and children. The bitter cold and tremendous amount of effort needed for their trek had sapped the strength from all three of them.

Fortunately, the seven Hunkpapa women – the Hunkpapa were known to be the stoutest of the

Sioux tribes – were now helping to organize the rescue. A couple of them went scrounging through the wreckage of their camp and secured knives or hatchets. They shook snow from the branches and felled small trees. After stripping the limbs, they tied animal hides or robes in place and made several travois. Upon these litters they put the lone elderly man and divided up eight of the smaller children. They next secured the passengers with strips of rawhide, cut from the fringes of buffalo robes. When the last child was in place they announced they were ready to go.

Louis led the way and the march to stave off certain death began. Dutch plodded along with the women, while Jess brought up the rear. However, Dutch foundered almost at once laboring hard to keep up. He stumbled and fell several times. Each time it was harder to regain his feet until at last, he could go no further. Louis stopped the procession, but Dutch lifted a hand in protest.

'Leave me!' he called to his dear friend. 'Save the women and children!'

Jess and Louis made their way to him, but they were both near exhaustion and had not the strength to carry him. It was all they could do to keep from collapsing themselves.

'We aren't leaving you,' Louis told Dutch.

'You have to keep going or we'll all die!' Dutch

said. 'Louis, you have to show the way. You can't be burdened with me.'

'Come on, old-timer,' Jess chided him. 'You were talking about us younger guys not being worth our salt. Get up and we'll see who is still on his feet when we reach the trading post.'

But before Dutch recovered enough stamina to try and stand, the Indian women made a decision for him. They moved two children from a travois and placed them on different litters. In about two minutes flat Jess had helped one of the woman strap Dutch to a travois. He was to be pulled by the durable and stout young woman they had revived first at the camp.

Jess was amazed at the Herculean effort of these Indians. The Hunkpapa women waged a furious battle against the wind, the blowing snow and mountainous drifts. Except for the small portions of food provided by the three-man rescue party, they had not eaten in two days, and they had lain next to death only hours earlier. But these were Indian women, strong in heritage and hearty by necessity; it was not in their make-up to quit.

Moving in a tight group, the seven women trudged forward like powerful draft horses pulling a deep-cutting plow against a stubborn virgin field. Louis fell down several times – each time helped back to his feet by one of the women. The wind hammered at the group, ruthless and cruel, gusting so hard it occasionally overturned a travois, but the group persevered and kept moving forward.

Jess checked with Dutch to keep him awake, but he had lost most sensation in his body and it was a fight to remain conscious. Quite suddenly, one poor young woman was blown right away! She, her travois and two babies were all swept over the side of the hill and out of sight. Jess took several steps in her direction to help but went down to his hands and knees. His lungs burned from sucking in the cold air; his fingers and toes were frozen stubs that refused to work; and his eyes grated like rusted balls in dry sockets. He collapsed in a heap, lacking the strength even to raise his arm.

The other Indian women moved close together, huddled with their backs to the wind and waited. They called and shouted to the lost member, words with no meaning to Jess, but full of hope and encouragement. Jess suffered a grim despair which engulfed his very being. They still had at least a mile to go. What chance did they have, mere mortals pitted against the unyielding power and overwhelming fury of the storm? They were all doomed to frozen graves in this endless sea of white death.

His gloom was suddenly shattered as an excited cheer arose from the Indian women. Jess lifted his head to see the lost young squaw had reappeared, her shoulders bowed against the bite of the wind, pulling her travois with the two babies back on board. Her face was a mask of grim determination, her teeth clenched against the ferocity of the swirling crystals of ice. Her gritty, never-say-quit valor stirred an inner emotion to life in Jess, a reserve energy he didn't know he possessed. The sight of her bravery and the unwillingness of the Indian women to give up, flooded his very being with a burning pride in humanity.

Jess cursed his weakness of the moment and rose to his feet. He yelled a cheer for the woman's resolve and pumped his fist into air. With a renewed determination, he turned into the teeth of the icy wind.

'You ain't got us beat yet!' he shouted. 'Not by a long shot, you don't!'

The three Indian braves hurried out from the trading post to help the children and one old man inside. Jess and Louis carried Dutch into his room and covered him with warm blankets. It was extremely crowded in the small trading post, but the fire warmed the near-frozen bodies and the severity of the frost was soon calculated. A number of small amputations were needed, including the removal of four of Dutch's toes – the task professionally done by one of the Hunkpapa women. Remarkably, there were no life-threatening cases among the hearty Indians.

As for Jess and Louis, they came through the ordeal with only mild cases of frostbite and tired aching muscles for the next couple days. The supplies ran low, but they made do with dried beans, a little bacon and pone or gruel. To the nearly starved Indians the meals were feasts.

The storm subsided and clear skies returned. It was on the sixth day after the blizzard when Jess spied four riders. He called out to Louis and soon many of the Indians were filing outside to greet Chief Strikes-the-Ree. He had arrived with three of his hunters. He explained a fourth had gotten lost from the group during the blizzard and, after spending the storm in what shelter they could find, his frozen body was discovered on their return to camp.

The hunting had not been great, but the chief had enough meat to tide his people over until they could set out again. He was extremely thankful to Dutch and Louis for saving his people.

Louis did most of the talking and used sign when words failed him. There was a lengthy exchange about how the chief could repay him and Dutch, and the stranger who had helped. After a time, the conversation ended and the chief gathered his people for the trip home.

Jess had not spent a lot of time with the women and children. He and the braves had worked each day to remove snow and keep a path clear around the trading post entrance and also the corral and lean-to, where his horse had weathered the worst of the storm. However, he had not tried to learn any of their words, nor had they shown interest in learning English. Everything was done through sign language. Even so, all three men stopped and gave his arm a grip, a sign of friendship. One of the women – he remembered she was the one who was blown over the side of the hill – also paused in front of him. He had noticed her within the confines of the room, but never had the opportunity to speak to her. She was a comely maid with sparkling, polished oak-colored eyes and a demure way of never meeting his gaze. She had kept pretty much to herself, other than tending to the children. She was slighter of build than most of the other squaws. For the first time since the storm, she made actual eye contact as she was leaving. She didn't reach out to take his arm, but did give him a slight nod of her head.

'Pleasure meeting you, ma'am,' Jess said, offering up his best smile. 'You and the other women showed me a strength I never knew existed.'

Oddly, there appeared a minute glimmer in her eyes as if she understood at least the intent of what he had said. She did not smile, but she did give him a second nod. Then she followed along with the others, returning to their home to salvage what they could and rebuild their camp.

With the Indians gone, the storm having passed and enjoying some welcome bit of sunshine, Jess and Louis did some digging out around the trading post and dislodged snow on the roof to remove some of the weight. They were jaded from the strenuous work when they finally stopped for the evening meal.

An unfamiliar silence lingered, a quiet not heard since the arrival of the three frozen Indians. Jess sat at the table with Dutch and Louis for a meal of beans and a thin gruel made of flour and water. It had been seasoned with salt and sprinkled with a little cheese. Louis called it skilly – Jess thought the definition of the word probably meant *the last meal before starvation.* Even with a little sprinkle of cheese, he could only eat it by sopping up some juice from the beans to moisten it first.

'I seen you giving the old flirty eye to Pale Flower,' Louis teased Jess after a few bites. 'She is a sweet little gal.'

'You mean the Indian girl I spoke to?'

'Yes, she worked for us some last summer, helping tan and clean hides. The chief traded her labor for salt and sugar . . . sometimes flour or tobacco. She would work a few days and he would pick out supplies to cover her wages. She's smart as can be, able to understand what we needed her to do without much instructing.'

Dutch bobbed his head. 'She does understand

26

more than a man would expect. I taught her a few words in English and Louis here has done the same. Don't remember her ever saying a word in reply though.'

'She once told me 'no' when I tried to lend a hand one time,' Louis advised them both, grinning at the memory. 'She's the only one in camp without a man.'

'There's more women than men in most of the Indian camps,' Dutch explained to Jess. 'Some chiefs take three or four wives, but many times those are widows who have no hunter to provide for them. I don't know how Pale Flower gets by.'

Louis said, 'She tends to the fires and works like she does for us I suspect – doing whatever she's told. I think the chief considers her like he might a younger sister or some such thing. I really don't know.' He shrugged. 'Fact is, we don't know much about any of them. They will share their camp, but not a lot about their family history.'

Dutch added, 'Only thing we know for certain is they consider the girl to be bad medicine.'

'Bad medicine?'

The man chuckled. 'Tell him what Two Toes said about her, Louis. He is the one Indian Louis talks to the most and he sometimes gives us a little information we can't get from the other members of the tribe.'

'What did he say about Pale Flower?' Jess wanted to know.

'He claimed she is a walking menace,' Louis explained. 'As a girl she accidentally sent fire to the chief's teepee. Then while washing some clothes, she was frightened by a bear and managed to cause a stampede of the horses from camp. It took two days to catch up all the mounts again. Another time, while helping with the cooking, she mistook a herb and added it to the pot during a meal . . . made everyone in camp sick.'

'Mistakes of youth,' Jess defended her. 'Those things could have happened to anyone.'

'When she turned courting age, the brave who was going to take her for a wife was killed during a buffalo hunt. A year later, a second brave chose her for his own and was promptly killed during a skirmish between the tribe and some northern Arapahos. After that the men in camp gave her a wide berth.'

Before Jess could defend those things as coincidence, Dutch pointed a finger at him. 'You know the avalanche that buried the camp?' He uttered a grunt of disgust and waggled the finger. 'They sure enough blame Pale Flower for that.'

'You're not serious!' Jess cried.

'Yup, if there is no rain and the streams run dry, it's her fault. If the stream floods and they cannot get across, it's also her fault. She's a dark cloud that hovers over the camp – bad medicine.'

'It's the way it is, Jess,' Louis clarified. 'The gal gets the blame for anything that goes wrong. Been that

28

way for as along as I've known the tribe.'

Jess felt sympathy for the unfortunate Indian girl, but there wasn't anything he could do about it. So he turned to other pertinent matters at hand. 'How are you two going to get by?' he asked. 'Feeding twenty extra mouths for several days has wiped out your store of goods. Do you have enough to get by?'

'The chief promised to drop us off some meat after their next hunt,' Louis replied. 'As for the rest. . . .' He lifted his hands in a helpless gesture.

Dutch was more optimistic. 'We have some hides ready for resale and spring always brings some travelers through. We've got a little tucked away for buying supplies, so we should make it all right.'

'I'd like to pay you something for my room and board, but I don't have any money till I get to a bank,' Jess told them. 'I earned a fifty-dollar bounty a short while back, but payment turned out to be a pay voucher and I need a bank to cash it.'

'You don't owe us for being neighborly, and there's a bank at Granville, about thirty miles due east.'

'Thanks, Dutch. With the weather clearing up, I'll mosey over that way tomorrow, if I can get through the drifts.'

'Never did ask what brought you here in the first place,' Louis commented. 'We aren't nosey sorts, but we've been together for a spell now and you never said a word about your business.'

'Bounty hunting isn't a business to be proud of,' Jess informed them. 'After the war, I ended up out of work, without a dime to my name. I happened to see a fellow who was on a local Wanted poster – he was part of a gang – and so I turned him over to the law. When I got paid, I picked up a few more handbills and thought to make myself a stake. I got lucky a second time with a tough *hombre* and earned enough to keep searching for other wanted men. This pay voucher I'm carrying was from the third man I brought in. I just never got a chance to cash it.'

'Why not?' Dutch asked.

'I've been following a gunman known as Prince. He is worth two hundred dollars – nearly twice what I've earned from the other three. With that much money, I could start myself a business or small ranch.'

'Seems I heard of that fellow,' Louis spoke up. 'Cold as a block of ice, a real killer, so the story goes.'

'He's wanted in two different states, but he killed a Deputy US Marshal and that got him on a federal dodger. They offered the big reward for his hide.'

'Pretty dangerous, looking for a man like that,' Dutch observed.

'Yeah, but it's about all I can find this time of the year. I looked around for work as I passed through Colorado and Wyoming, but the ranch jobs were shut down for the season. I don't know of any other work to keep from starving.'

Louis perked up, as if struck by a sudden notion. 'You're *that* Jess Logan!' he exclaimed. 'You brought Bloody Bill Gates in alive! I remember hearing about that.'

'Can't say it was a lot of cunning on my end,' Jess admitted. 'The man was so drunk he couldn't stand when I found him.'

The two men laughed and Louis said, 'That sure isn't the way the story in the newspaper went. Made out like you had to wrestle him like a bear and only won the fight because you outlasted him.'

Jess grimaced. 'Like I said, I'm not proud of bounty hunting, but it's the only profession I can earn a living at for the time being.'

Dutch rubbed his chin thoughtfully and said, 'There's one job I know of hereabouts and that is at the stage station over at Lakota Crossing. Ether Boyle and Harry Beaumont run the place. They had a nephew helping out but he got an itch to seek his fortune elsewhere and took off for the big city.' Dutch heaved his shoulders in a shrug. 'Don't know if it would pay more than room and board, but it's better than risking your life chasing a killer like Prince.'

'I never drove anything bigger than a hay wagon or buckboard. Do you think they'd hire me?'

'Not much driving involved, other than making a trip for supplies on occasion. Most of the work is tending to animals and changing teams,' Louis said.

'We would offer you a place here, but it barely supports us.'

'Louis is right,' Dutch agreed. 'You showed your worth by going out and helping save the lives of those Indians. Ain't but a handful of men who would have done that, especially with you being a stranger to this here part of the country. If you had offered to stay here at the store and look after the three braves, we wouldn't have thought any less of you for it.'

Louis added, 'Yep, there's no reason in the world why them or us should have survived an ordeal like that . . . but we did.' He puffed up with pride. 'We brought every one of those people here safely and you stuck with us all the way. You proved your mettle.'

'Thanks, fellows. And I appreciate your hospitality, I sure do.'

'If you're worried about Harry and Ether,' Dutch offered, 'I'll jot them a note and set them straight about you. I wager they'll give you a shot. You can start over at the crossing and let someone else chase after those jaspers on the wanted posters.'

Jess had a hard time finding his voice. 'That's durn nice of you two. I mean it.'

'It's like Louis said, we'd keep you on here, but we are going to be on a steady diet of skilly by the time spring arrives.'

'Thanks again, Dutch . . . Louis. I'll sure do those fellows a good job; you won't regret vouching for me.'

CHAPTER THREE

Wayland Lott sat at the table with Prince, Sax and Delaward. They were playing cards for peanuts . . . literally. It had been lean pickings since the end of the war. Money was hard to come by and many of the flood of pilgrims owned little more than the clothes on their backs. Lott and Saul Ackers had scratched out a meager existence over the years, but they were on to something big this time. Hence the joining up with three more men.

Ackers entered the saloon and made his way over to their table. He sat down at the empty chair and kept his voice low.

'It's here,' he whispered, 'a lieutenant, five armed guards and a driver.'

'What about the transfer?' Lott wanted to know.

'Tomorrow or the next day. They are going to follow the stage route and stay at Colby Junction one night and then another at Granville.'

'How do they look to you? Do we have enough men?'

Ackers grinned. 'There's the driver, but the five riders are as green as unbroke mules. The lieutenant has some seasoning, but you know most of the regular army boys went home after the war ended. The detail guarding the wagon are raw recruits and they've had to fight their way through drifts every step of the way. They intend to spend a couple days resting here before starting again. Should give us plenty of time to get set for them.'

'Still say we would be better off robbing the stage,' Sax offered. 'One lonely guard as opposed to six horse soldiers and a driver.'

'Yeah, but the stage is carrying practically nothing,' Delaward put in. 'The army payroll is cash wages for a couple hundred troops.'

'And they will chase us to the ends of the earth if we take it,' Sax argued. 'We're talking over ten thousand dollars – maybe twice that!'

Lott waved him to silence. 'Ackers and I have been doing jobs like this for fifteen years and never been caught! We have a plan that will work and we won't leave any trail to follow. It's all mapped out. By the time the army realizes the payroll is late at the fort, we'll be halfway to San Francisco.'

'You're sure about them stopping at Lakota Crossing?'

'It's the only way station between Granville and the Kansas border. The troop will have solid protection at the next two stops, but there's nothing at Lakota Crossing for fifty miles in any direction. There won't be anyone to see what happens and no telegraph either.'

'Stages only use the way station at Lakota Crossing a couple times each week,' Ackers informed Sax. 'Probably less with the weather being so bad lately. With the army's present schedule, we'll have a two or three-day head start before anyone even knows what has happened.'

'I still say seven troopers won't be easy.'

Prince showed a rare smile. 'If you want out, you can leave at any time, Sax.'

Sax paled under the man's deadly gaze. Prince had all the warm emotions of a snake. He was a man born without a conscience, able to kill without giving it a second thought. Quick on the trigger, he actually seemed to enjoy watching someone die.

'No . . . I'm only saying how I wish it was a stage. You know how it is, a man likes to look at every side of a problem.'

'Studying too much will be the end of you one day, Sax,' Prince breathed the words quietly. It reached each man's ears at the table like the silent hush of death.

'It's already settled,' Lott said, breaking the icy

spell. 'Ackers is going to ride ahead and get a look at the way station. We'll stay a day in advance of the soldier boys, so when we join Ackers we will have a full day or two to prepare for the supply wagon.'

'It's a good plan,' Ackers said. 'I'll get an idea of how to deal with whoever is running the station while you boys make sure those blue-bellies keep on track.'

'So when do we get started?' Prince asked. 'I've got a manhunter on my back trail and he's one scary son.'

Lott snickered. 'Who would dare come after you?'

'Ever hear of Bloody Bill Gates?'

'Everyone has heard of that crazy killer. Story goes he kilt his own father when he was fifteen. Then he raised hell all during the war, while a good many men were off fighting. Butchered whole families, so I've heard.'

'Even if all of the tales aren't true,' Ackers put in, 'he has put no less than a dozen men in their grave in the past two or three years. The man was a rabid dog without any conscience. We heard he was hanged a couple months back.'

'Yes he was, and this bounty hunter, Jess Logan, he took him in alive and all by himself. You can't blame me for being a little nervous, having the man responsible for capturing Gates sniffing my trail.'

Sax emitted a low whistle. 'I don't blame you one bit. I sure wouldn't stick around and try my luck against the man who took in Bloody Bill Gates.'

Ackers put on a confident look. 'Not to worry. I'm leaving today and you can move out with Lott and the others tomorrow or the next day. Once the job is over, you can get lost in any city you choose and live like a king.'

'We'll be a day back of you,' Lott assured Ackers. 'If something happens, we can get in touch with you.'

'The sooner this is over the better I'll like it,' Prince said.

'Good luck,' Lott offered, watching his long-time friend leave the saloon.

'This is it, boys,' he said, after Ackers had left. 'We're going to be rolling in money when this is over.'

'Lessen we get kilt first,' Sax grumbled. 'I still say seven soldiers won't be no picnic.'

'We'll handle them just fine,' Lott assured him. 'We only have to take over the stage station and they'll ride right into our trap. Them boys will be under our guns before they know what hit them.'

'What if they fight back?' Sax lamented. 'We could end up dead real sudden.'

'They will have been riding for twelve hours,' Prince dismissed his worry. 'Those boys will be cold and stiff when they arrive. They sure won't be ready to battle against five guns.'

'See?' Lott spoke to Sax. 'There's nothing to worry

about. It's why we chose the Lakota station stopover, so they would be tired from a long ride and half-frozen from the cold. You'll see, it's all going to work out fine.'

Sax begrudgingly gave a nod of his head. A couple men at the way station and seven troopers still sounded like a big undertaking for only five men. But he was in on the deal now. There was no backing out. He would set aside his fears and do the job. With any luck, it would be the first and last robbery he would ever pull.

Morning brought a clear sky and sunshine. The air was crisp and the deep snow's frozen crust was hard enough to support a man's weight in places. Jess checked on his horse and broke the ice in the watering trough. Once the animal was tended to he rolled up his bedroll and stuck his few belongings into his saddle-bags. He would have liked to stick around another day or two and let the trails melt off, but his two gracious hosts were nearly out of supplies. He hadn't even taken breakfast, so as to leave more for the two hospitable trading post operators.

The arrival of two Indians interrupted Jess's short walk back to the house. He recognized the one on horseback as a brave who had been with the chief's hunting party. The second was on foot, the rather comely – yet supposedly bad medicine – Indian girl,

Pale Flower. She had a heavy blanket wrapped around her shoulders and about her head to ward off the cold. Frosty crystals of ice were encrusted to her clothes, with only a small portion of her face showing. She came forward to stand a short way from the door to the trading post.

'Hello,' Jess greeted the two of them. 'Didn't expect to see you back so soon.'

The Indian gave him a blank expression. Pale Flower had eyes only for the toes of her snow covered, knee-high, moccasins.

'You're here to see Louis and Dutch,' Jess surmised, walking to the front of the trading post. The Indian remained wooden, while Jess pushed open the door and called to the two men.

Dutch, limping from his loss of toes, and Louis came out of the trading post to greet the pair. Louis communicated with the brave through a mix of words and sign. After a moment, the Indian removed a quarter of venison from the back of his horse and passed it to them.

There was a second exchange between the two, although the Indian spoke with mostly short grunts and a few gestures. Louis showed surprise at something being discussed and they bantered back and forth for another short spell.

'What's going on?' Dutch asked his longtime friend. 'Has Pale Flower come here to work off some of the chief's debt?'

Louis finished a last communication with the rider before he looked over at Dutch. Even as the brave swung about and rode away, he laughed.

'What?' Dutch demanded to know. 'Tell me!'

'The venison is to help hold us over until the chief can go hunting again. He knows we used up all of our provisions feeding his people.'

'All right, the chief is an honorable man. What about Pale Flower? Is she supposed to work for us?'

'Not exactly.' Louis chuckled and pointed at Jess. 'The chief gave her to our young friend for helping to save the lives of the women and children. She now belongs to him.'

Jess felt his mouth fall open but was too dumb-founded to re-close it. He looked inanely at the girl, who appeared to accept her fate calmly.

'Belongs . . . to me?' he muttered stupidly. 'That can't be. I'm not looking for a wife or servant.'

'It's a little late to worry about that, son,' Dutch told him. 'Once given, a gift from the Sioux can't be returned.'

'But . . . but I haven't got a job or a place to lay my head. What am I supposed to do with her?'

'The chief isn't being all that gracious,' Louis informed him. 'Pale Flower has no man, no one to provide for her. They have more mouths than they can feed at the camp. And then there's the girl's reputation for causing calamities,' he winked at Jess. 'Chief Strikes-the-Ree is repaying your help and bravery with a gesture that will also help him and his remaining people. Remember they think the girl is bad luck.'

Jess scowled at the two men. 'This is plum crazy. The girl isn't a horse to be traded or given away!'

'I don't know what to tell you, son,' Dutch said. 'The chief has given her to you. She has no home to go back to.'

It was a ludicrous situation. Jess turned and put a serious look on Pale Flower. 'It's your life, ma'am. You ought to have a choice,' he said firmly. 'What do you want?'

She displayed surprise. He wondered if she understood what was happening, or was she even capable of making a decision on her own. After a brief hesitation, she made sign – a subtle hand gesture indicating she would go with him.

'That settles it,' Louis said, working hard not to smile. 'She's yours now, whether you like it or not.'

'She's a purty little gal and a hard worker,' Dutch joined in. 'Most Indian braves would give a half-dozen horses for such a fine wife.'

'This ain't no joke!' Jess yelped. 'How can I take care of a woman? Goldurn it, boys! I'm doing a fairly lousy job of taking care of myself!'

'You might come across another band of Sioux,'

Dutch suggested, growing serious. 'If you were to approach them with an offer, they might be willing to take her off your hands.'

'How about you two?' Jess was growing more desperate by the minute. 'You said she helped you with the hides and such. Couldn't she work for you to earn her keep?'

'You don't understand.' Louis was no longer smiling. 'The girl is yours. It's not something we can change. If we were to keep her here, the chief would think we were throwing his present back in his face. It would be a mortal insult. If an Indian happened to be killed by a white hunter or something, he might allow we could be killed to get even. We are pretty much forced to keep the bargain he's made for our own safety.'

'But I don't have a horse for her,' Jess complained. 'My mount can't pack double through these hills. With the drifts and such, it'll be a chore to get through myself.'

'Indian women seldom ride a horse,' Louis said. 'She'll walk along behind you, the same way the squaws and children walk behind the braves whenever they move their campsite. It's the only form of travel most of them have ever known.'

Jess groaned. 'Are you sure there isn't something else we can do about this? I mean, I'm not looking for a slave.'

'You can ride too fast for her to keep up and maybe lose her,' Louis said in a cool voice. 'Once she decides she will never catch up or find you, she would probably try and survive by herself.'

'Wouldn't last long out in these mountains alone,' Dutch contributed, making the point crystal clear. 'But you'd be rid of her that way.'

Jess stared at the girl. She showed no emotion, her eyes hidden by dark lashes, while she kept her head lowered. 'I would never do that, not to anyone,' he said. 'I'm more concerned for her welfare. I don't have a way to survive the winter myself, not unless your pals over at Lakota Crossing give me a job. And what do I do with the girl if they do hire me?'

'Take her with you to Lakota Crossing,' Dutch suggested. 'Pale Flower is a good worker and understands a little English. I'll bet Ether and Harry will let her earn her keep right alongside of you. They would be getting two workers for the price of one.'

'Yeah,' Louis said, 'and then if someone comes along who needs a woman for whatever reason, you can likely trade her for something of value.'

'I'll gladly set her free, but I'm not going to trade her like I would a horse,' Jess replied bitterly.

Dutch gave him a curious look. 'I thought you fought for the Confederacy – to keep slavery in this country.'

43

'I fought with my Texas friends to allow Texas and all the other states to make their own rules without big government telling us what to do,' he explained. 'Me and a lot of boys I fought with never did hold with slavery.'

'Well, want her or not, she's your responsibility now. She will follow you until her strength runs out.' Dutch grinned, 'And you've seen a sample of her fortitude.'

Resigning himself to being stuck with a companion, Jess gave in. 'All right, I'll take her with me, at least until she can make known what she wants. It would sure help if I spoke her language.'

'You can make her understand by talking and making a little sign,' Louis chimed in. 'She's a smart one, that gal. We seldom showed her how to do anything more than once and she would do the job right.'

'It's still not fair for her,' Jess argued.

'There's nothing you can do about that; an Indian woman has limited choices in life. Pale Flower will do whatever you tell her. She's your woman now.'

'Thanks,' Jess said drily. 'That makes my life so much easier.'

He saw Dutch and Louis exchange looks. They didn't wink and laugh, but he knew they felt this was quite a humorous situation.

They wouldn't think it was so funny if the chief had given the girl to them!

44

CHAPTER FOUR

Once Jess was out of the mountainous terrain, the snow, having been blown off of the flatlands and back into the foothills, was only a few inches deep. It didn't take any longer than that before he had his first encounter with the headstrong Pale Flower. He stopped when he reached the main trail, dismounted and motioned for the girl to get aboard.

She gave a negative shake of her head.

'Come on, lady,' he coaxed. 'We can make better time and my horse has been growing fat and lazy for the past week.'

She didn't move.

Jess put his hands on his hips to confront her. 'Look here, Pale Flower, we need to get to Granville before the bank closes so I can cash my pay voucher. Otherwise you and I are going to be eating tree bark for supper and burrowing into a snow drift to spend the night.'

She remained stationary, ten feet back of his horse, as if not even a stick of dynamite could move her.

'Goldurn it!' He finally used a gruff tone of voice. 'You either do as I say or I'll have to leave you behind. I'm not going to starve or freeze to death because you are too stubborn to cooperate. We've got to reach Granville!'

She frowned at him for a long moment, then took a hesitant step forward. 'That's right,' he coaxed, 'come over here.'

Pale Flower moved slowly over to stand by his mount. Jess patted the back of the horse behind the saddle. 'This is where you will ride,' he told her.

She hesitated, as if ready to make a hasty retreat, so he swiftly put his hands on her waist. Before she could shy away, he lifted her up, swung her around and placed her on the horse. He ducked his head so his hat would hide a smile that surfaced from seeing the surprised look on her face. It made him wonder if she had ever sat astride a horse before.

Jess mounted by stepping into the stirrup with his left foot, but twisted and rose up with his right leg forward so he could swing the leg over the neck of his horse and take a seat in front of Pale Flower. When he started the horse moving along the trail, the girl chose to hold on to the cantle of the saddle rather than put her arms around him.

'I suspect you aren't much for talking,' he said over his shoulder, 'but it helps to pass the time.' And he proceeded to tell her about his home, the war, and how his parents had left to start life anew. He told her how he had roamed for weeks on end, working at a farm or ranch for a meal or two, shooting game or catching fish, anything to get by. Then, by chance, he had recognized a man from a wanted poster and collected a bounty when he and several others were captured. A short few weeks later, he had searched out and caught a second man. With a voucher for a third man, he had set his sights on the one with the highest bounty and followed him to Missouri. Now the trail would be cold and he needed to land the job at the way station. It would get him through the winter and he could decide what he was going to do come spring. When he had brought her up to date, he glanced back at her.

'What about you, Pale Flower?' he asked. 'How did you end up with no one in your life?' She didn't answer. Then he hadn't really expected her to. 'What do you think about being given away to a man you don't even know?'

After a lengthy silence, Jess turned to other subjects – the weather, the type of work he might expect at the stage station, even his concerns about the future and what lay ahead, especially now that he had her along.

As Jess had no provisions they didn't have to stop for a meal, but continued to ride until he picked up the main trail. There were tracks showing that a wagon or stage had been along in the last day or two. From that point on they made good time. They reached Granville at late afternoon, yet before the bank closed. It was a crossroads town with a lot of travelers, and there were also farms in the surrounding area and even a nearby slaughterhouse. As such, there were several businesses and two saloons, with a hotel and café.

There weren't a lot of people on the street, but those who were took notice of a man riding into town with an Indian girl riding behind his saddle. Some glances were curious, others more hostile. There had been trouble with many of the Indian tribes ever since a battle in Colorado at Sand Creek a couple years earlier. Although that attack had been against the Cheyenne, many other tribes saw it as an act of war against all Indian nations and they had retaliated.

Jess ignored the onlookers and rode over to the bank hitch rail. The business was not much for size, located between the jail and the saloon, which Jess thought was convenient – borrow to gamble, lose your money, get into a fight and then be escorted to jail, all within a couple hundred feet.

The walks, where they had been built, were mostly

clear of snow. Mounds of dirty white sludge and snow were piled in the alleyways and next to the walks. The sun was out, but it was not warm enough to melt the snow.

Jess swung his leg over the neck of his horse and slid to the ground. He turned and reached up for Pale Flower. Instead of cooperating, she pushed back and slid over the rear end of the horse, landing on her feet without his help.

'You wouldn't want to do that with a good many horses,' he warned. 'Champ is broke well enough that he doesn't mind that kind of dismount, but some animals would kick you into next week.'

She paid no attention to his words, pulling her blanket tight and crossing her arms for warmth.

'Come on,' he said, leading the way into the bank. Pale Flower followed two steps behind, but did enter first when he held the door open and gestured for her to get inside the building.

Jess felt an instant heat from a pot-bellied stove, standing in one corner of the sparsely furnished interior. Within the room, the bank had a short counter, a bit higher than the bar table at most saloons, enclosed in a wire and wood frame with a single window for dealing with patrons. Other than that, there was a single writing table and no chairs.

'You warm yourself while I do my business,' Jess instructed the girl and motioned toward the stove.

She didn't argue this time, but stepped closer and spread her hands in front of her to warm her fingers.

Jess decided she would do what she was told whenever she happened to be in agreement with the order, and walked over to the teller window.

'First time I've ever had a Sioux Indian in here,' were the man's words of greeting.

'Long story,' Jess didn't explain her presence, passing over the reward payment. 'Can you cash this pay voucher for me?'

He studied it for a moment. 'Sure, I've seen one or two like this before. We will honor it for a charge of five per cent. You understand, the fee is because we have to forward it to the original bank in order to get reimbursed.'

'I guess that's fair,' Jess said, though it seemed like the bank or company issuing the voucher should be the one to pay for any fees. Still, he was broke and needed the cash.

The teller had just finished counting out the money to him when something bizarre happened. There came a gasp – like surprise or shock – from Pale Flower. Jess began to tuck the money into his pocket and glanced her direction. The girl's eyes were wide and a fiery determination swept across her face. She searched the room frantically, threw off her blanket and grabbed the shovel used to clean out the clinkers and ash from the bottom of the stove. Then she bolted for the door, yanked it open and raced outside.

'What the hell got into your squaw?' the teller asked.

Jess didn't answer, but collected Pale Flower's blanket and followed after her. Once outside the bank, he looked up the street in time to see the girl run up behind some guy who was apparently headed for the saloon. He stopped dead in his tracks, aghast, as she clouted the man on the head with the shovel!

Even as his senses returned, and he started again in her direction, a man with a badge appeared at the doorway of the jail. Pale Flower ignored everything and everyone, furiously striking the surprised victim over and over, using both hands to gain power with her swings. The lawman bolted forward and slammed into the girl with a body tackle. They both landed in the middle of the street.

Jess arrived as the lawman pinned Pale Flower to the ground. He tore the shovel from her fingers and gave a quick look at the injured man. The victim had been knocked to his knees by the first blow and remained there with arms flung over his head for protection. He had lost his hat, revealing a thick mane of hair, held at the back of his head in a single braid with a strip of rawhide. There was a streak of blood on the side of his face from a scalp laceration and one ear had turned a dark purple.

'Don't hurt her, Marshal,' Jess spoke to the lawman. 'The lady is with me.'

A fellow from the saloon had come out to see what was going on. The marshal pointed at him and said, 'Sid, take this guy over to the doc's place. Then let me know how he is.'

The man paused to spit a stream of tobacco juice before answering, 'You got it, Renny.'

Jess watched as Sid helped the injured man, lifting him up to drape his arm around the man's waist. The two of them crossed the street looking like a couple of drunks after a hard Saturday night.

'All right, you feisty little Indian squaw,' Renny grated the words through clenched teeth. 'I'm going to let you up, but you're under arrest and coming with me. You understand what I'm saying?'

'She understands a little English,' Jess told him.

The marshal gave Jess a 'who-the-hell-are-you' kind of look, but removed his weight from Pale Flower. He kept a tight hold on one of her wrists and pulled her to her feet. Without a word to Jess, he led her into the jail.

Jess followed after them and, once inside the office, he handed the girl's blanket back to her. She was still breathing hard from exertion and accepted the robe without meeting his eyes.

'What was that all about, Pale Flower?' He asked her. 'Who was that man and why did you attack him?'

She ignored his questions, her face a mask of stone, refusing to look at either him or the marshal.

Renny was of medium build, probably in his thirties, with a shaggy head of hair and a bushy mustache. His sideburns reached to his lower jaw and he had the face of an abandoned hound dog. Even so, there was an honesty in his make-up. His chest heaved with his effort to control his ire and he glowered at Jess.

'Look, whoever you are, this here Indian gal assaulted a man right in front of my jail. She's going to spend some time behind bars if you don't give me a damn good reason for her attack.'

'Honest, Marshal, I have no idea.'

'How did you end up with a squaw?'

Jess told him the short version of how she had been a gift for his help. He also told him the girl understood a little English, but she had not spoken except in sign to him.

'You best get her to give sign as to why she attacked that man,' Renny warned Jess. 'Either that or she's going to end up sentenced to jail for thirty days - that's the usual punishment for assault – and it means she'll be cleaning the streets and gutters to pay for her keep.'

Jess sighed, knowing this would be a waste of time. 'I'll give it another go, but the young lady is a bit on the stubborn side.'

'Yeah? Well, she ain't the only one,' the marshal said with some force.

Jess tried again, asking Pale Flower please to tell them why she had attacked the man. Did she know him? Was he a bad man? Did he make some kind of gesture or insult her in some way? Had he ever hurt her?

Each question got the same silent response. She offered up not a sign or word in her own defense.

'What are you doing in town?' Renny asked, once he grew tired of the complete lack of progress.

Jess explained about the pay voucher and how he had to cash it before heading over to Lakota Crossing, where he hoped to land a job. When he told the marshal his name, the man eyed him more closely.

'Jess Logan, the man who brought in Bloody Bill Gates?'

'It wasn't as hard as you might think,' Jess told him candidly. 'The guy was drunk on his duff and couldn't even stand up.'

Renny grinned. 'Some men would take more credit for capturing a butcher like Bill Gates.'

'I'm not looking for a reputation.'

'I know the two ex-hunters who run the station at Lakota Crossing,' Renny said, getting back to the present. 'They took over the station back when the war started. Most of the young men went off to fight and they were the only two hermits who would put up with living fifty miles from the nearest saloon or outside company.'

'Dutch said they used to have a nephew who worked for them, but he had moved on.'

'Yeah, only met him a time or two, but he enjoyed being around people and gambling. The solitude out there about drove him crazy. You figure a stage once or twice a week is their only contact with the outside world, other than a monthly ride here for supplies.'

The door opened and Sid appeared at the entrance. He entered the marshal's office with a perplexed look on his face.

'Well?' Renny asked impatiently. 'How's the victim?'

Sid was working on a chaw of tobacco about the size of a fist. He had to wedge it over snug against his cheek with his tongue before he could even speak. 'He left,' he said, spraying a few drops of brownish spittle.

Renny glanced with disfavor at the fresh drops of juice on his floor, but stuck to business. 'What do you mean – he left?'

'The doc said being hit with the shovel only bruised him some.' Sid paused, looking for somewhere to spit. Seeing nothing at hand, he held back the juice and slobbered ahead. ''Cept for splitting the skin around his scalp, the guy blocked most the blows with his forearms . . . and he was wearing a heavy coat.'

'And you're telling me he didn't want to stick around to make a complaint against the woman who attacked him?'

'Nope. He gave the doc a dollar for cleaning and bandaging the scalp wound and skedaddled.' Drool seeped out of the corner of Sid's mouth, so he wiped at it with the back of his hand before finishing, 'I seen him headed for the stable, so I reckon he's gone by now.'

'You get his name?'

'Said it was Joe Smith. He had rented a room at the hotel, but he must have changed his mind.'

'Sounds like a phony name,' Jess surmised. 'And him not wanting to see you face to face, Marshal – the guy could be on the run from the law.'

'You bounty hunters think everyone is on the run.'

'Why else wouldn't he stick around?' Jess asked. 'The man was attacked and beaten . . . without provocation, as far as we know. Why would he shrug it off unless he didn't want to face you? And what about him renting a room and then leaving town?'

'Said he had some place to be,' Sid explained, spraying the floor again from his giant wad of chew. 'I guess it must have been more important than spending the night here in Granville.'

'Thanks, Sid,' Renny said. 'Now get out of here

before I have to clean up your tobacco juice with a shovel!'

Once the man was gone, Renny directed Pale Flower into a cell. He closed the door and used a key to lock her in.

'You don't think that is necessary do you?' Jess asked. 'I mean, the girl has been as quiet and peaceful as a dove until she saw that man. He had to have done something to her or someone she knows.'

'Unless she is willing to tell me about it, I'm holding her for assault.'

Jess studied the girl for a few moments, but her dour resignation remained intact. She moved to the single bunk, wrapped her blanket around her shoulders and sat down.

'I don't know a lot about the law, but I do know you can't charge a person with assault unless you have a victim. Your victim left town.'

Renny snorted. 'Well, smart guy, even if I can't get her for assault, I can sure enough charge her with disturbing the peace. I myself witnessed that.'

Jess did some quick thinking and moved away from the cell. Drawing the marshal out of earshot from Pale Flower, he said, 'I can't hang around town while she is locked up for a couple weeks, Marshal. And I can't leave her here with no place to go. Can't we find a way to settle this?'

The lawman waved a nonchalant hand. 'Judge

usually gives a lawbreaker ten days or ten dollars for disturbing the peace. I don't see why he won't do the same with the gal.'

Jess took in the information without comment. 'All right,' he said. 'I've got to put up my horse and see about a room for the night. What about getting the girl something to eat?'

'I'll provide her a chunk of bread and a cup of water,' Renny said. 'That's all prisoners get.'

Jess shook his head. 'I'll bring her something to eat, once I get settled.'

'Being that you're going to do that, Logan, you can bring me something too. Etta Mae's Eating Emporium serves my meals. Ask her to make me up my usual plate when you get your food.'

Jess bobbed his head. 'OK, I'll see you in a while.'

Renny followed him to the door. 'Tell Etta Mae to send me some dessert too,' he said. 'The town doesn't pay for anything other than the "daily special". I have to eat the special every damn day or else I have to pay extra. Only benefit I get is she throws in whatever they're serving for dessert.'

Jess gave a bob of his head. When he opened the door, he saw the girl look up. Her eyes widened at seeing him leaving and her mouth opened. For a brief moment it appeared she might speak or call out to him. However, she quickly lowered her gaze to the floor and held her silence. Stepping through the exit he felt a cold blast of wind and was thankful he had enough money to get a room.

CHAPTER FIVE

The doctor had given Ackers a couple sips of laudanum for the pain, but his head and ear both throbbed and the breeze was an icy chill that cut through his heavy coat and numbed his face, hands and feet. Even so, he dared not stick around Granville, because of the marshal. There might be some Wanted posters lying about with descriptions of him and Lott. Plus, he wasn't about to wind up explaining to a lawman or judge why he might have been attacked, especially when he had no idea of the reason. It was hard enough to tell a convincing lie; when a man didn't know the truth it was twice as hard!

He heard someone say his attacker was an Indian girl. He and Lott had killed quite a few Indians over the past dozen years. He didn't get a good look at the squaw who had attacked him, but she must have recognized him from one of their murdering parties. He grunted at the notion. Served him right, getting a beating, if he and Lott had been careless enough to allow one of those red devils to survive an attack.

He stared upward at the setting sun. He couldn't stick with the plan and go to the way station because it was too far away. His only route was to head back to meet up with Lott and the others. Foregoing a check at the station shouldn't make a difference. The five of them would have to ride in blind and then decide when and how to take over the place.

He and Lott wanted this payroll. They had grown tired of small-time robbery and theft. They were getting too old for living on the run, hiding in caves and sleeping under makeshift lean-tos, always on guard for fear of being recognized. This was their big chance and they had a good team for the job . . . with the possible exception of Sax. He didn't have the sand of a good bandit or thief. He had never killed a man, but was eager to make a pile of money and forget his four years of fighting against the Confederacy.

Delaward was a quiet sort, strong as a longhorn steer and a good shot. He was the kind who took orders without question and could be counted on in any kind of fight. He had killed some banker's son in a bar fight – broken the man's neck. Whether it would have been ruled self-defense or not was a question, but Delaward had run. When Lott and Ackers first met him, he was removing rocks from farmland for fifty cents a day. That was a job he never wanted to go back to.

Prince considered himself a gunman, a loose term that had floated around since the coming of the penny dreadfuls – short fictional books of Wild West adventure and gunfights. He was quick to get his gun out of its holster, that much was no story. And he boasted to the killing of a dozen men . . . though it was more likely two or three. Ackers let him claim what he liked, so long as he did his job. Being an expert shot was what they needed to get this job done. Seven troopers were escorting the wagon. If it came to gunplay Prince was sure to kill his share.

Ackers pulled the collar of his coat tightly up under his chin. It would be a couple hours past dark before he reached the settlement at Brown's Flat. That's where he would meet up with Lott and the others.

He thought back to his beginning with Lott. They had both started out as buffalo hunters some fifteen years back, and Lott had happened along to save him from dying at the hands of a couple of angry Arapaho. He had sold them some whiskey, the likes of which he had brewed himself with a makeshift still. The alcohol had been green and toxic. A few sips didn't hurt, but the Arapaho had drunk way too much, causing the death of three Indians and blinding another. He would have been killed but for Lott arriving to shoot the two Indian braves.

A month later and the two of them began raiding small wagon trains or lone travelers. They were a good fit, as neither wanted to be tied down with a job or family. Plus Lott didn't mind a killing when things went bad. Both of them knew, if they were ever captured by the law, they would hang. It was incentive not to get caught, and also to find a target that would allow them to leave the country and never look back. This was their one chance to hit the bonanza and no one was going to mess it up . . . least of all some crazed Indian squaw.

Jess had the hostler feed his horse a double ration of oats and then give him plenty of hay and water. He also paid to have Champ rubbed down. It was an extra two bits, but the game little gelding had packed double all day and they needed to cover fifty miles come morning. After some haggling over price, he bought a bony packmule, a thick saddle blanket and bridle, all for twenty dollars.

Once he had a hotel room, he put up his few belongings and went over to Etta Mae's Eating Emporium. The food didn't look all that tempting, but a starving man couldn't be choosy. When he ordered his dinner, he told Etta Mae about the marshal asking her to make up a plate for him, and how he also needed a second for the prisoner. He did remember the dessert and it came as something of a surprise.

'You're joshing me,' he said. 'Ice cream? In the middle of the worst blizzard anyone has ever seen in these parts?'

'The blizzard is over,' Etta Mae replied in a droll tone of voice. 'Besides, it ain't like I can get apples or currants for a pie or pudding this time of year.'

Jess liked ice cream but not when he was already frozen to the bone. He finished his meal and nixed the idea of dessert for himself. However, he did take a dish along for both the marshal and Pale Flower. With a tray balanced on one hand, he opened the door to the jail and quickly stepped inside to escape the frigid night air.

'Mr Logan!' a female voice exclaimed.

He blinked in surprise seeing a welcome relief on the girl's face. She hid the emotion at once, but he realized she had thought he had left her behind.

'Well, say!' Renny spoke up from his chair behind his desk. 'The little squaw can speak when she's of a mind to.'

Pale Flower was passive again, but she covertly watched Jess's movements.

'Here you go, Marshal,' Jess said, sitting a bowl of stew on the desktop, followed by a small dish of ice cream and eating utensils. Then he carried the tray over to the cell.

There was an opening for passing food and water to the prisoner, so he rested the tray on the horizontal bar. 'Supper,' he informed the girl.

She came forward hesitantly, took the tray back to her cot and sat down. Then a strange thing happened. Without so much as looking at the stew, she picked up the spoon and began shoveling ice cream into her mouth. It was as if she had been waiting for that single dessert all of her life. She appeared to savor each mouthful and the ice cream disappeared so quickly he thought her head would explode from the numbing pain, the kind he had felt a time or two when eating something cold much too fast.

She didn't lick the dish, but she did make sure she had gotten every last drop. Then she began on the bowl of stew, making short work of devouring it too.

'Looks as if your little squaw was about starved,' Renny noted, once she had cleaned both bowls.

'Yeah, I hadn't eaten since yesterday . . . and they didn't have a lot of food in her camp. I doubt she has eaten much of anything in at least that long.'

'Now what?' Renny wanted to know.

Jess retrieved the tray from Pale Flower and went to the marshal's desk. He added the two dishes from his supper to the tray and lowered his voice.

'I'll take care of this, but I need for you to keep

her here overnight.' Before Renny could offer up a response, he continued. 'The guy at the hotel said he don't allow Indians, and the livery has several men who've paid to sleep out of the cold already. If that fella Pale Flower attacked, Joe Smith, had not skipped town, there wouldn't have been a room for me either. I was lucky enough to get the room he had already rented.'

'Times are hard,' Renny said. 'This blizzard put an end to about every kind of work there is. The men with money are holed up and everyone else is just trying to survive. Look at me, forty dollars a month, two meals a day over at Etta Mae's place and I sleep here. And even though I'm a town marshal, I'm expected to settle disputes twenty or thirty miles away in any direction. I can't afford a deputy, so when I'm stuck with a prisoner, I have to watch over him for his entire sentence, twenty-four hours a day.'

'It sounds pretty tough for so little money.'

'Yeah, the coal to heat this place costs me ten dollars or more a month. Then there's feed and stable for my horse – I feel lucky if I have a dime left over on payday.'

'You mentioned a fine for the girl?'

'Ten dollars is what the judge usually charges someone who disturbs the peace.'

'I need to get started at daylight,' Jess told him. 'It's a long hard ride to Lakota Crossing, and the mule I bought might not even make it that far. Can we get the judge to settle this issue tonight?'

Renny chuckled. 'The judge is likely floating up to his eyeballs in whiskey by this time. He don't usually find the floor with both hands before noon.'

'That'll be too late,' Jess said. 'How about I pay you ten dollars for the fine and another dollar for letting the lady sleep in the cell for tonight. You can explain to the judge about how I had to leave early and give him his half when he is up and around.'

Renny smiled. 'Now that's a plan I can live with. An extra dollar's worth of coal would sure help me get through this here cold spell.'

'Then we have a deal?'

The marshal stuck out his hand. 'She's yours first thing in the morning.'

'Thanks, Marshal, I do appreciate it.'

Jess took the tray and went to the door. He shot a look Pale Flower before making his exit. A lost and confused look was on her face, but she quickly lowered her eyes so he could not read what it meant. In the next moment, he was outside, feeling the bite of the wind, hurrying over to Etta Mae's so he could return the dishes. Then he would stop by the general store and pick up a few things. After that it was off to bed. He would need a good night's rest before tackling another fifty miles of frozen ice and snow. He certainly hoped he wasn't making the ride for nothing.

Seeing Jess leave, Pale Flower experienced a sinking sensation inside her chest. He had brought her a meal, but was he coming back? He hadn't wanted her – he had said as much at the trading post. Dutch and Louis had even told him how he might trade her or be rid of her some other way. He hadn't said goodbye, but this was his chance to be done with her.

The emptiness invaded her being a second time. She hadn't spoken up or offered any explanation for her attack on Ackers. Did Jess take that as an act of declared independence? Did he think her silence meant she didn't want him involved in her life? He and the marshal had shaken hands as if it was farewell. What if he never returned? She fought down the fear of being deserted. She would make do and get by, she always had.

Back to her present situation, she hated being locked up like a wild animal. Of course, her behavior was little better than an animal. She hadn't thought about the consequences, her action had been on a primal level. She had seen the face of a killer and all reason had deserted her. Her only impulse was to shoot, stab or hit him with something. Unfortunately, as she overheard from the man who took him for treatment, Ackers was not seriously hurt.

She groaned silently at her failure. The small

shovel had not been a decent weapon. She should have grabbed the gun from Jess's holster and taken off running. By the time he had caught up with her, she could have put an end to the murdering snake.

Deciding to try to sleep, she took the single blanket from the cot and added it to the one she carried with her. She lay down on the bunk and pulled and tucked the blankets tight about her. The marshal added some black rocks to the stove and poked around with a long, straight piece of iron. He seemed satisfied after a few moments and walked over to the door. After slipping a wooden bar in place and securing the entrance for the night, he doused the lamp.

'Sweet dreams, Little Squaw,' he said.

She didn't reply, but listened as he removed his gun belt and boots. Then he sagged down on his own bed . . . which was much closer to the stove than the cot in the single cell. If he kept the fire going all night, she would be comfortable and warm for the first time in weeks.

Yes, now if only I can shut off my brain and actually go to sleep.

She wondered again if she should have told Jess about the killer, Ackers. She felt certain he would believe her, but what could he do? Ackers was a white man and she was the unwanted squaw to a man who collected bounties. She did not know much about such things, but a bounty hunter had once come by the trading post while she was working there. The man had continually leered at her, disrobing her with his eyes, molesting her with vile looks and lustful intentions. He had bragged about a man he had killed, though it had been for a small reward. After he had left, Dutch and Louis had said what a despicable sort bounty hunters were.

Closing her eyes tightly, she wondered if she would ever see Jess again. He had watched her eat her dinner with an intense curiosity, but he had said nothing. When he left, the shaking of hands with the marshal looked as if some kind of agreement had been reached. She could only wonder what it meant for her.

The burning in her eyes threatened tears, but she firmed her resolve. She had been alone for so long . . . so very long. Perhaps that was why it hadn't hurt her feelings when the chief had suggested she be made a present to the wandering stranger. The attempts to wed her to two different members of the tribe had both ended in tragedy, and all of the families were hard-pressed to feed and clothe their own. Now, after the destruction of the camp and the loss of several in their tribe, there was no longer a place or provisions for her among the Hunkpapa.

Her present fear was that Jess might have turned her over to the marshal, intent upon leaving her there. The two men had talked about her being imprisoned for the attack on Ackers, but she did not know for how long. And the man with the tobacco had said Ackers had left town. Did that hurt or help her situation? She just didn't know.

I should have spoken up, she admonished herself again for not explaining about the murdering cut-throat named Ackers. Had she done so, perhaps Jess would not have forsaken her.

CHAPTER SIX

'What the hell happened to you, Ackers?' Lott asked, seeing the bandage wrapped about his forehead and the discolored left ear.

'Change of plans,' Ackers grumbled, dismounting at the livery stable. 'I got waylaid at Granville by some Indian squaw. I didn't dare stick around and have the marshal come snooping into the why for, so I lit out and came back here.'

'Good thinking,' Lott said. 'Best not to be recognized by anyone. We don't want some marshal getting curious before we pull this job.'

'Where are the others?'

'Prince is over at the casino with Delaward, and Sax went to get something to eat. I told him I would join him, but I wanted to check on the horses first. I couldn't believe it was you when I seen you coming down the street.'

'You've good eyes – always did get around in the dark like a cat.'

'I wasn't sure until you passed that nearest lighted house. Then I recognized the way you sit a horse – always did ride like a sack of spuds.'

Ackers grinned, got down from his animal and began to loosen the cinch. 'Sorry about changing the plan. If you think it's for the best, I'll light out at daylight. I could still make the crossing a day ahead of you and the boys.'

'No, we've still got our ace in the hole, as far as the soldiers go. The stage station is something we'll take care of when we get there. I doubt it holds any surprises.'

'Help me put up my horse and I'll join you and Sax. I'm for a meal and then a bed for about sixteen hours of sleep.'

'Yeah, you look like you were mauled by a bad-tempered grizzly.'

'Never even got a look at her,' Ackers told him. 'The first bash came from behind and dimmed my lamps till I couldn't see. The doc said she could have killed me if she'd have hit me with a heavier weapon. I heard someone say she was using a clinker shovel.'

'Too bad we don't know where she came from, in case some of her people are nearby.'

'The marshal put her in jail. From the chatter back and forth between the guy who took me for treatment and the doctor himself, it sounded as if she was alone and would be spending the next couple weeks behind bars.'

'Good, that means she'll be out of the way when we ride through.'

'We still need to be on the lookout. The marshal there takes his job seriously, but I got out of town without him seeing me. I doubt there's any cause to worry.'

'Bur-r-r-r,' Lott shivered, 'Let's get your horse put up and head for the eating house. It's colder than a well-digger's rump out here.'

Ackers grunted his agreement. 'I'll second that notion. I'll have to warm up a few degrees to become an icicle.'

Jess awoke while it was still dark, took a few minutes to shave and wash up, then shoved his few belongings back into his saddle-bags and tossed them over his shoulder. He picked up the package of items and a coat he had purchased at the store, tucked them under his arm and headed for the livery stable. The hostler had set his things out so he would not have to wake him. It took only a few minutes to saddle his horse and have the packmule ready for travel.

The eating places were not yet open, but he had picked up some hard tack and a couple sweet rolls to hold them until they reached the way station. The early morning chill felt as dense as walking through a shower of ice, but the sky was clear. It would likely warm up to near freezing during the day.

Jess rode Champ and led the mule to the jail. Dawn was breaking when he tapped lightly at the marshal's door. There was a bit of grumbling before the bar was removed and the door cracked open.

'When you say daybreak, you mean daybreak, don't you?' Renny complained.

Jess entered and closed the door while Renny went over and put a match to a lamp. Then he turned around and waited, his hand extended. Jess passed over the eleven dollars and Renny stuck them in his pocket. Jess wondered if the judge was going to get his share of the fine, but it was of no consequence for him.

Rather than going to the cell himself, Renny gave Jess the key. 'She's all yours,' he said. 'I hope she doesn't decide to go after you like she did that guy yesterday.'

The girl was sitting upright on her bunk, both alert and awake, when Jess put the key in the cell door. She folded and draped her blanket over her arm. By the time he worked the cell lock open she was on her feet. He pulled the door wide open and she burst through it like his long lost love!

Pale Flower threw her arms around him and hugged him so tightly he couldn't breathe. 'Mr

Logan,' she murmured softly, 'you came for me.'

Renny roared loudly with mirth. Jess looked helplessly at the marshal as the man sat down, looking all the world as if he would split a rib from laughing. 'You wanted her,' the marshal taunted him. 'You sure enough got her!'

Pale Flower finally stepped back. There wasn't a lot of light given off by the solitary lamp, but Jess was certain the girl was blushing.

'Uh, we'd better get going,' he stammered. 'It's a full day to Lakota Crossing.'

She stood ready while he gave a wave to Renny. 'Be seeing you, Marshal,' he said. 'If I get the job, I'll likely be in to pick up supplies on occasion.'

'I'll keep an eye out,' Renny grinned, 'for both of you.'

Jess went out into the brisk morning air, with the girl right on his heels. He stopped at his horse and pulled down a heavy woolen jacket he had picked up at the store. 'Put this on,' he told Pale Flower. 'It's not much for looks, but it'll be warmer than the blanket by itself.'

The girl did not argue, slipping on the much-too-large coat. The sleeves covered her hands, but that would help to keep her warm. While she adjusted her blanket so she could protect her neck and ears, he made sure the heavy saddle blanket was secure.

'You'll ride the packmule,' he informed her. 'It

should be more comfortable than riding behind me.'

Again, no discussion or argument. She moved up and accepted his help getting on the mule. Once seated, she waited for him to get aboard Champ.

'Let's go see about that job,' Jess said. 'I'm about broke.' With a grin, 'Funny how much faster a man's money goes when he's got a woman around.'

Pale Flower smiled. It was not exactly a humorous display, but more as if he had said something very flattering.

They reached the stage stop as the sun was setting. The land was open to three sides with a small range of hills to the east, rising up beyond the corral. Jess surveyed the large barn, a sturdy-looking shed, and a sizable shelter which had been constructed in one corner of the corral to protect the animals from the harsh elements. There were several draft horses and two mules milling about inside the large enclosure. He also spotted a coop for chickens and a pen with several pigs.

The station house was fairly large, as it had to accommodate the feeding of passengers from the stage. A one-room addition, with it own chimney, had been added to the original structure, probably for extra housing.

Jess pulled up at the hitch rail at the front of the house and dismounted. He looked at Pale Flower.

This time, rather than getting down by herself, she waited patiently for him. He moved over to the mule and placed his hands on the girl's waist and helped her down. She stood uncertainly for a moment, likely shaky from not being used to so much riding and also numb from the cold. Once she appeared to have her bearings, he let go and stepped away.

For the first time since he had met her, she looked at him squarely, candidly. It was a little startling for Jess as she had dark chocolate eyes, set beneath modest eyebrows, and her gaze was inclusive and quite bold. He wondered what she was thinking, but the door opened and the moment was lost.

'Howdy, stranger,' a man greeted them. 'What'cha got there with you, your own little squaw?'

'Long story,' Jess replied. 'I was told you might have a job open.'

'Could be,' the fellow answered back.

Jess removed the letter Dutch had sent to introduce him. He stepped forward to meet the speaker and a second man who had come out to the porch. Somewhere around fifty years of age, both men were grizzled, with bushy mustaches and brows. They were nearly the same height, with each carrying a little extra weight around his middle.

The one had more gray in his hair and he took the letter. After a short read, he smiled at Jess. 'I'm Harry Beaumont and this here is my pard, Ether Boyle.'

'Jess Logan,' he returned the introduction, 'and this is Pale Flower.'

'Well, son,' he said jovially, 'we can certainly use the help. But Dutch must have warned you the job don't pay for squat.'

'Room and board is more of a concern than money for the winter,' Jess admitted candidly. 'And I've got the young lady to think about. Dutch and Louis claimed she is a good worker. I'm kind of looking after her for a spell.'

Harry nodded his understanding. 'We've only got one spare room. Built it for my nephew, when he was working for us, but he has since moved on. Got himself a job driving stage.'

'Ain't much for comfort,' Ether added, 'but it does keep you off the ground and out of the cold. It's the addition on the north side of the building. It has a fireplace, so you don't freeze at nights.'

'I'd sure appreciate the job. I'm a fair hand with horses and I can get fresh meat soon as the weather clears enough to hunt.'

'If Dutch vouches for you, it's good enough for me,' Harry said. 'Put your animals in the corral with the others and come inside. We've got a kettle of stew simmering in the pot – same as we had yesterday, but we don't cook much unless we're expecting a stage to come through.'

'You don't have anything against Indians?' Jess

checked with the two men. 'I mean, I know there's some who don't care for having one around.'

'She's your concern, not ours,' Ether commented. 'If she can help with cleaning or cooking, that's all the better for us. When we have a load of passengers arrive she can help with the food or stay out of sight. Shouldn't be any problems that way.'

'I'm much obliged for the chance to work for you men,' Jess said. 'I'll sure do you a good job.'

'Put up your hoss and bring in your gear,' Harry offered. 'I'll stoke up the fire enough to heat up the kettle of stew.'

Jess led his horse and mule to the corral and stripped off the gear. The shed was only a few steps away and he discovered belts, straps, wheel parts, plus some other tack and tools. He dumped his saddle and blanket but kept the package and saddle-bags. He was not surprised that Pale Bird had stood passively by and waited for him.

'You should have gone in where it's warm,' he told her. 'I'll bet you're about froze.'

Rather than make sign or try to speak, she stepped back so she could follow him to the house. He stopped at the door and held it for her . . . which caused some delay to her entering. Finally, at his beckoning to her, she went inside so he could close the door behind them.

The main room was spacious, with a long table

and a bench on either side. It looked as if it would serve about eight-to-ten people. The pot-belly stove was in the front corner and put off a comforting amount of heat. Jess took Pale Flower by the hand and walked over to stand next to it.

'Glad we got here when we did,' he spoke to Ether, who was the closer of the two men. 'I've about lost feeling in my hands and feet. A person might freeze in the saddle after dark.'

'Warm yourselves a few minutes, while the stew heats up,' the man offered. 'I'll go in and start a fire in the spare room. We've been keeping the door closed since the blizzard. No need heating up space we weren't using.'

'I saw some tracks of a wagon or something on the road,' Jess mentioned.

'That was from the coach to Kansas City. It made its first run since the storm. The old whip who drives the stage told us he saw the bodies of a good many animals and several graves along the route. That last blizzard is the worst storm I can remember.'

Jess told them about the Indian camp and how all of the Indians had nearly perished. He nodded at Pale Flower as he finished. 'This little gal is the one who helped me get through it. I was flat on my stomach, ready to let the cold take me, when she come marching over a crest of ice and snow, pulling a travois with the two little kids on it. It was seeing her determination that got me back on my feet.'

'No one lives a harder life than an Indian woman,' Harry interjected, from where he was giving the stew a stir.

While he and Pale Flower ate, Jess learned what was expected from him. It would be his job to tend the animals and horses. He would also be responsible for having the teams ready to trade out when the stage arrived. Other chores would be to hunt fresh game, collect and chop wood, repair harnesses and maintain the corral, barn and animal pens. In all, he would do most of the physical work around the place, while Harry and Ether would handle the station duties and see to the meals and needs of the travelers and stage-line employees.

Pale Flower would help with the cleaning, do some of the cooking and handle the laundry chores to pay for her keep.

It was an hour past dark when the two men bid them goodnight. Pale Flower followed Jess into the small addition and waited for him to tell her what to do.

The small heating stove had taken some of the chill out of the room, but the floor of the addition was dirt, and there was little respite from the icy wind. It seeped through cracks in the walls and penetrated the room from the frozen world outside.

There was a bed, some hooks for hanging clothes

and a small dresser with four drawers. It must have been bartered from some pilgrim travelers at one time, as there was a child's doll painted on the bottom drawer and the image of a toy soldier on the top. The bed frame was built from wood and the mattress was packed straw under a canvas liner. It was about half again as large as an army cot. Three blankets were folded at one end and a single pillow was at the other.

'We'll have to share the bed,' Jess told Pale Flower. 'There isn't room for me to sleep on the floor.'

She frowned and gave her head a negative shake. Then she went to the corner of the room and sat down, leaning against the wall and crossing her legs. She pulled the blanket tight around her shoulders as if prepared to spend the night in such a position.

'No, that isn't going to work,' Jess told her firmly. 'I won't have you catching pneumonia or getting frostbite from trying to sleep like that.'

Another frown.

'Look, I'm not going to touch you, I promise. And we'll keep our clothes on, if that is what worries you.'

The stubborn look remained in place.

'It's the cold,' he pleaded for her understanding, 'we have to bunk together to keep from freezing. We can't feed wood to that pitiful little stove all night. We'd use up a winter store of wood in less than a week.'

No change in her stance.

'Either you agree to share the bed or I'll go out and spend the night in the barn.' He rubbed his hands together as if to warm them. 'And I'll darn well freeze some of my favorite body parts if I have to sleep with my horse.' He sighed. 'Plus Champ snores something awful.'

To his surprise, the girl uttered a partially suppressed giggle. He stared at her agape, but she did not make eye contact.

'You understood that, didn't you?' he queried. 'You understand more English than Dutch and Louis ever expected.'

The humor disappeared at once.

'And that ice cream you had last night – you've had it before. I saw the way you gobbled it down. When did you eat ice cream? It's not an Indian treat.'

She didn't respond to his observations or questions, but rose to her feet. As he stood back and watched, she began to make up the bed with the blankets, adding her own on top when finished. She sat down and unlaced her knee-high moccasins. Her feet were encased in stockings, probably some from the trading post, and then she lay down next to the wall.

'Come,' she said, waiting to pull up the covers.

Jess turned out the room's only lamp, kicked off his boots, hung his gun, jacket and hat on the hooks on the wall and laid down next to her. She pulled up the covers at once and turned her back to him.

The bed was bigger than some but still a snug fit for two. However, the warmth from the young Indian soon penetrated through his outer clothing. Jess smiled in the dark. Sleeping next to her certainly beat any campfire he had ever managed. He wondered if she felt the same way.

CHAPTER SEVEN

Jess was awake early and slipped out of bed. Before he could get his boots on Pale Flower was folding up the blankets and placing them on the bed.

'You don't have to get up yet,' he said, putting a match to the room's only lamp.

'Men say Pale Flower work,' she said without looking up.

'You seem to understand a lot of English.'

The girl paused as if thinking about something. 'Dutch and Louis teach,' she clarified.

He grinned. 'You're a puzzle, but you do keep a man warm at night.'

'Better than horse?' she asked coyly.

'No contest,' he told her, laughing at the first bit of humor she had shown him.

Both Harry and Ether were up by the time Jess had stoked the stove in the main room. There was a reason for their rising early.

'Ether will show you the hows and whats concerning the chores, whilst I will give your little squaw the tour of the kitchen and show her where we keep the cleaning stuff and the like. With any luck, we'll have something cooking on the stove by the time you two finish up with the animals.'

Jess put on his coat and tugged down his hat, while Ether got bundled up. Harry led Pale Flower into the kitchen and began to show her around.

'Ready?' Ether asked.

'Let's get it over with,' Jess said.

'If it warms up some you might try to get in some hunting one of the next days. We are running low on meat, although we still have a fair store of flour, sugar and beans.'

When they stepped outside, Jess discovered it was daybreak and the sky looked clear. If the wind didn't come up, it might be warm enough to start melting the snow. He mentioned as much to Ether and added: 'If we don't get another storm, I can probably go looking for game tomorrow.'

'There's often some deer over near the northern foothills. They come down to water along the river there. Might find some sage hens or rabbits among the trees too.'

'Sounds promising,' Jess said.

The chores were wrapped up in short order. The

pig pen held a sow and four young, but they wouldn't be butchering size for some time. There were only six chickens and they had managed four eggs between them. Ether joked how they seemed to take turns laying so none of them qualified for the roasting pan. There was bundled grass and oats for the horses, but they wouldn't need as much feed once the snow was gone. From early spring until the heavy winter storms they turned the animals to pasture, except when a stage was due to arrive.

As Harry had promised, the smell of food being cooked greeted their return to the house. Pale Flower was frying eggs and strips of venison in two different skillets, while Harry was fussing over the coffee.

'That pard of mine likes his coffee to be black as a moonless sky and thick enough for a frog to squat on without sinking.' He laughed. 'I usually pour myself a cup before it has time to harden into a block.'

'I tend to favor my coffee a little thinner than axle grease too,' Jess said.

The meal was mostly eaten in silence, other than Ether and Harry discussing where there might be a little game for Jess to hunt the next day. The blizzard had driven the animals to shelter, and the storm was so severe that many would be near starving. Game birds and animals would be trying to find food along the creek and lower hills, which were clearing, while the mountain regions would still be mired by deep drifts.

Jess mostly listened to the two men, as they had lived here for years and knew the best areas to hunt. Ether wished he could go along, but he didn't sit a horse well after taking a fall the past year. As for Harry, he didn't have the eyes for hunting, able to see close up, but not far away.

When they had finished breakfast, Jess chose to clean and oil his rifle and pistol. He wanted everything ready for his hunting expedition. He spent most of the morning getting his gear lined out, while Pale Flower finished in the kitchen and then began to clean the interior of the cabin. It was a major chore as it didn't appear much cleaning had been done since the place was built.

The two old partners chose to spend much of the day playing cards and talking about their youth and things they had seen over the years. Jess decided it was going to be an informative – though possibly boring at times – day at the station.

Ackers found Lott sitting at the back of the saloon alone. The other three men were at a table playing poker. Pulling up a chair Ackers sat down next to his friend.

'We best not sit around here any longer. The payroll arrived an hour or so ago and things have changed. They are only going to spend the night here, then tomorrow night at Granville and on to Lakota Crossing the following day.'

'What the hell!' Lott exclaimed, sitting up straight. 'I thought they were going to rest up a couple extra days.'

'The lieutenant moved up the schedule. If we leave now, we can make Granville tonight and still arrive a full day ahead of the soldier boys.'

Lott tossed a dollar on the table and stood up. 'All right. We don't want the shipment to arrive before we're set and ready.'

'We leaving?' Sax spoke up, having heard the two of them talking.

'Grab your gear and meet over at the livery in ten minutes,' Lott told the three men at the card table. 'Our timetable just got moved up.'

'Suits me,' Delaward lamented. 'I ain't had a decent hand all damn day.'

'Good thing we weren't playing for real money,' Prince sneered. 'You'd be pulling this job for free . . . 'cause you'd owe it all to me.'

'Get a move on, boys,' Ackers gave the order. 'It's thirty miles to Granville and it's not much fun stumbling along a slush-crusted trail in the dark.'

As the three men filed out, Lott and Ackers went to their shared room to pack. Once behind the closed door, Lott put a hard look on Ackers.

'You're sure nothing is in the wind?' He appeared nervous. 'This is a big take – biggest thing we ever tackled. We can't afford any mistakes.'

'It's nothing. The lieutenant is the one who decided to pick up the pace. He's got himself a girl back at the fort and wants to get back to her before she gets too lonely. As far as the payroll goes, they still think the story of transporting regular supplies is holding solid. We'll catch them napping when they ride in and that'll be it. You and I will take our share and head for California.'

'That sure sounds good,' Lott approved. 'You know, I've heard tell it don't ever snow in some parts of that state.'

Ackers began to stuff his few belongings into his war bag. 'After this last blizzard, I sure wouldn't miss ever seeing that white stuff again.' He paused from packing and looked at Lott.

'You fill in Sax on the details about the ambush yet?'

'I told him we are going to lock everyone in a storage shed. I hate to think how he might react if it comes to shooting.'

'Might be better not to have him along.'

'He's the one we'll send out to meet the wagon,' Lott explained. 'If he catches a bullet during the exchange. . . .' He shrugged.

'And the boys know to leave the driver to me?'

'They'll have enough to keep them busy and everyone has been told the man holding the reins is your responsibility.'

Everything was ready and the two men left the room. Both men were filled with a growing excitement. This was it, the big haul, the single job that would set them up for life.

Pale Flower was tired from the long day's work. She entered the small addition after she finished clearing the table and putting away the dishware from the evening meal. One step into the room and she stopped dead in her tracks.

'Thought you might like to do something most women enjoy,' Jess said, nodding toward the tub. 'I used the stove to heat water for you to take a real bath.'

A look of puzzlement entered her face.

'Don't worry, I'm not staying in the room while you bathe,' he told her quickly. 'You can set something in front of the door if you want to insure your privacy.'

'A bath?' she breathed the words so softly he barely picked it up.

'The package on the bed is for you.'

She gave him an inquisitive look, then walked over to the bed. When she removed the store wrapping, she discovered it was a plain cotton dress – powder blue with white lace around the collar and sleeves – along with women's stockings and low-heeled every-day shoes. He had also included a simple hairbrush.

'White women's clothes,' she said uncertainly.

'Yes,' he said with a bit of smugness. 'Well, they didn't have any Indian maiden outfits at the Granville general store.'

She displayed her habitual frown.

'Go ahead and take the bath,' Jess told her. 'The water won't stay hot for long.' He pointed to the floor next to the tub. 'The soap and washing cloth are all I carry in my saddle-bags, and I would wager Ether and Henry don't have anything else for washing your hair. The bar of soap will have to do until we can get you some real shampoo. I think that is what they call a woman's hair soap.'

She remained stationary and said nothing.

Rather than let the water get cold, he raised up a hand in farewell. 'I'll leave you to your bath.' And he went out the door and closed it.

Pale Flower stood, staring blankly at the vat of water, trapped within a torrent of uncertainty and conflicted emotions. She recovered her faculties after a moment and stepped over to test the water. It was still quite hot and beguilingly inviting. Jess had arranged everything, even to the placing of a blanket next to the tub so she could wash her hair without having to kneel on the dirt floor.

Dismissing her hesitation she hastily removed her soiled clothes, piling them neatly on the end of the bed. When she stepped into the bath, a world of warmth caressed her skin. As she lowered herself to a sitting position, she welcomed the strange and wondrous comfort. Her baths had been washing at a creek or an occasional dip in a river or pond. This . . . this was heaven on earth.

Outside the door, Jess had listened until he heard the splash of water. Satisfied she was taking the bath he sought out Harry and Ether. They were sitting by the fire and munching on pine nuts.

'I need to talk to you fellows about something,' Jess opened the conversation.

'Sit yourself down, sonny,' Ether offered. 'What's on your mind?'

'It's about Pale Flower,' Jess said, taking a chair a few feet away. He told them about buying her regular clothes, then explained how she had attacked a man in Granville and beaten him with a small shovel. 'She wouldn't tell me why, but there's no doubt she had a great hatred for the man.'

'She don't look the sort to get violent,' Henry said.

'I don't for a minute think she would ever attack anyone coming into the station, but I thought you ought to know about it.'

'She's got something of a mystery about her then?'

'Like I said, I don't know the answers yet.' He

sighed, 'And I don't know how long it will take to get the whole story.'

'We understand, son,' Henry assured him. 'Do you have any idea about the guy she attacked?'

'No. I didn't get a good look at him. I have to think she witnessed him killing some Indians or something.'

'What do you need us to do?' Ether wanted to know.

'I just wanted you to know in case that same guy should happen to ride through here. Once I get the truth I'll pass it on, but it could take some time before she will want to talk about whatever happened.'

'Nuff said,' Ether assured Jess. 'We were intending to keep her away from visitors anyway, leastways when you're not around.'

'That's right, sonny,' Henry spoke up. 'Now that you've warned us, we'll do our best to shield her from any strangers passing through.'

'About her wearing the clothes I bought. . . .'

Henry waved a dismissive hand. 'We won't pay no particular attention – like we didn't notice the change. That suit you?'

'Yes, and thanks, fellows. I'm sure giving her some time and not asking questions will make it that much easier for her to deal with her situation. I expect one day she will tell us the story.'

'It's time we were getting to bed,' Ether said. 'You let the gal know that our asking her to stay out of sight of the visitors ain't because we're ashamed to have her around. It's for her own good.'

'Like my pard says,' Harry agreed. 'We'll see you two in the morning.'

Jess thanked them both and returned to his room. He waited some minutes outside the door and listened, but there was no sounds on the other side. Finally, he put his knuckles to the door and tapped lightly.

'Come,' the girl's meek voice invited.

Jess entered to discover Pale Flower, wrapped in a blanket, standing next to the stove. Her damp hair dangled on to her shoulders. The tangles had been brushed out and an uneven fringe draped on to her forehead. Still wet, it was much more flattering than having her hair in braids.

'You're not dressed?'

She cast a meaningful look at her pile of dirty clothes. 'Need washing.'

'What about the dress?'

Her fixed expression and the negative shake of her head revealed she had no intention of wearing the new dress to bed.

'I don't understand,' he said. 'What are you. . . ?' The question died in his throat as she lowered the blanket enough for him to see she was wearing his spare shirt. As she was much shorter than he was the shirt draped down to her knees.

'I see,' he gulped awkwardly. 'So this is all you could think of to wear.'

A red hue tinted her tanned cheeks as she gave a slight nod. The shirt fit her like a blanket with a hole for her head. He might have suggested making her a sort of poncho for a sleeping gown, but it wouldn't have been much different from what she had on. He concluded the decision had been made.

'I got to say, that shirt never looked that good on me.'

The words caused the wisp of a smile to play along her lips.

'I think it will do just fine,' he said. 'And you don't have to worry,' he added, lying both to her and himself, 'I won't give how you're dressed a second thought.'

Jess put away the wash cloth and soap as Pale Flower spread the blanket she'd been wearing on the bed. Then she got under the covers. He intended to be a gentleman, but he did glimpse the shirt as it rode up above her knees. He looked away at once, immediately cursing the weakness of desire that rushed through his very soul.

'I'll just dump the water and come to bed. It's late and I know you must be tired,' he said to the girl. At the same time, he told his brain to stop replaying the vision of seeing her cream-colored legs over and over.

Jess dragged the tub from the room and through the main room to the door. He pulled it away from the porch before he dumped it, so the ice would not be along the main path. Then he stowed the tub away and hurried back inside. *Goldurn,* he thought, *it's going to be as tough as chewing cactus to get any sleep tonight!*

CHAPTER EIGHT

Rising a little before first light, Jess bundled up and went out to do the morning chores. By the time he got back, Pale Flower was dishing up some grits and toast for breakfast. She looked like a rancher's housewife moving about the kitchen area in the plain cotton dress. Her hair was loose about her shoulders and she had obviously used the hairbrush again. He enjoyed the new look and paused to admire the flowing mane.

The girl did not make eye contact with anyone, but he felt she was relieved that no one mentioned anything about her dressing as a white woman.

Henry and Ether gave Jess some last-minute ideas during breakfast about where he should hunt. When the meal was finished, Harry rounded up a pound of jerky and some hard biscuits, so Jess could take something along with him to eat.

Jess gathered his belongings, said farewell and went to the barn. He quickly put the mule on a lead rope, saddled his horse and packed his gear behind the saddle. He had taken most everything he owned, in case he bagged an elk or something and couldn't make it back to the station before nightfall. He wanted to be prepared for any contingency. Everything was secured and ready when he heard the sound of snow crunching underfoot. He turned to see Pale Flower. She hadn't bothered to put on her coat, with her arms crossed against the morning chill and already shivering.

'What's the matter?' he asked.

She ducked her head, hiding her expression. 'I . . . want to . . . to say goodbye, Jess Logan.'

He opened his heavy jacket and stepped over next to the girl. He put one arm around her and used the coat to help warm her from the cool morning air. She could have remained that way but chose to move in closer, pressing up against him so he could draw her inside his coat.

'I'll try to get back tonight,' he said, nearly overwhelmed by her nearness. 'I'm getting kind of used to having you around.'

'My tribe say Pale Flower is bad medicine – bad luck,' she murmured.

'I don't think you're bad luck. I think you are sweet as honey and about as cute as a newborn fawn.'

The usual, unfathomable frown drew her brows together, yet she regarded him with an odd scrutiny. He continued with a query, 'Is there something you'd like to tell me?'

She did not meet his gaze.

'Like how you speak such good English?' She hid her eyes beneath lowered lashes. 'And how you happen to know what ice cream is?' Now she ducked her head as if ashamed. 'Or why you attacked that man in Granville?'

She made not a sound.

He continued the interrogation. 'I tried real hard to be the proper gentleman last night, but I happened to catch sight of your legs below the hem of my shirt.' He felt her stiffen in his arms. 'Where you are protected from the sun, you have very light-colored skin. Is that because you aren't an Indian?'

The girl's head came up and she displayed an instant alarm.

He put on his most sincere expression. 'I think I've proved myself worthy of your trust, Pale Flower. Other than the one little peek last night, I've been a gentleman. I haven't tried to take advantage of you – even with you being given to me like property – and I didn't desert you at the Granville jail. I believe you owe me the truth.'

The girl seemed to wage an internal war for several agonizing seconds. At last, she sighed, having made a decision.

'I was ten years old, back in 1854, when cholera raged through the country. People were dying in Chicago, Cincinnati and most all cities of size. To escape the plague, my father took our family and headed to Boston, Massachusetts. From there, many settlers were heading west for Wisconsin, Nebraska or Missouri and Kansas.

'We left with a wagon and did fine until we reached a stretch of country beyond the Missouri border. That's when three men stopped our wagon to rob us.' She struggled with the words, the memory obviously still vivid in her mind.

'My father tried to bargain with them, but one of them got angry and shot him. My brother, who was fifteen, used our only gun and shot back. He killed one of them but the two killers, Ackers and Lott, both began shooting. They kept firing their guns until my mother and brother were hit several times each.'

She had to stop and take a breath to dislodge the emotion which blocked her words. 'I had ducked down and my mother fell on top of me. I lay there, frozen with fear, feeling my mother's warm blood soaking my dress. I knew I was going to die.'

Jess pulled her a little closer, offering her what strength and solace he could.

She recovered her grit after a few seconds and went on with the story. 'Before those two murdering animals could search the wagon, a party of Indians came riding up. They had heard the shooting and came to see what was going on. Ackers and Lott left the one robber where he had died and rode off.'

'So the Indians adopted you into their tribe?'

'There were no settlements nearby,' she told him. 'If they had left me at the wagon, I would have died. We weren't on a major road or trail and hadn't seen another wagon or house in two or three days. The Indians took me in and I was with them until you came along to save us from freezing in the blizzard.'

'They gave you to me because you were bad medicine,' he said, trying to lighten the mood. 'Could be you just weren't cut out to be an Indian's wife.'

'Chief Strikes-the-Ree would agree with you,' she replied.

'So what is your real name?'

'Regina Carlson.'

'I'm proud to make your acquaintance, Regina Carlson,' he said. 'You can call me Jess.'

'All right . . . Jess,' she said softly.

'Soon as I return, you and I are going to discuss your future . . . Regina.'

A timorous smile played along her lips and she leaned closer. 'I'd like that. Please come back safe.' Then she tilted her head back slightly, as if to look at him squarely, not an examination, more of a subtle invitation.

Jess set his inhibitions aside, compelled to taste those desirable lips.

Regina didn't balk. She readily accepted the kiss and gave a slight pressure of her own lips. The kiss was brief, yet warm and delightful. When they broke contact, she pushed gently out of his embrace and a faint smile tugged at the corners of her mouth.

'You're the first man I ever kissed, Jess Logan.'

He felt light enough that it was a wonder he remained earthbound. 'I'd like to think I'll be the last.'

'Could be,' she teased. 'We can talk about it when you return.'

He grinned at her. 'Like I said, I'll only be gone a day . . . maybe two, depending on the snowdrifts and my luck.'

'Goodbye, Jess,' she said. 'I'll be waiting for you.'

Jess watched as she turned about and hurried back to the warmth of the cabin. He smiled at the bounce of her hair and how she had to lift the skirt to run. He didn't know yet what the future held for him and Regina, but it would be her choice too. One thing was certain, he wouldn't trade or give her to another group of Indians.

It was mid afternoon when the five riders stopped on the main road. They were bundled up for the cold, but it had been a miserable night.

'Not a room to be had in Granville,' Lott complained. 'We ought to take our money – when we finish this job – and build us a big hotel. Durned if we wouldn't make a fortune during the winter months.'

'A dollar to bunk in the barn!' Prince added his ire. 'I've never paid a dime to spend the night in a loft before.'

'Yeah, and there wasn't much straw or hay to spread around neither. We'd have been just as warm sleeping in the snow.'

'That's why we left a full hour before daylight,' Ackers said. 'It didn't make sense to lie there freezing our tails off in that rotten barn.'

'Speaking of barns, looks like they built a pretty big one for the stage stopover,' Sax observed. 'Looks to be several draft animals in the corral too.'

'Remember the plan,' Ackers told the others. 'We don't want any trouble today. The supply train will be here tomorrow, so we'll be agreeable paying customers till then.'

'Don't worry,' Delaward sounded off. 'We know what to do.'

The five of them rode into the yard and stopped next to the hitching post.

From inside the station Regina looked though the solitary glass window. She sucked in her breath and gasped.

'There's men outside!' she called to Ether and Harry.

Her tone of voice was enough to alert both men. They came running to see what was the matter. She pointed out the window.

'They're bad men!' she explained quickly. 'Robbers . . . killers . . . bad men,' she stipulated firmly.

'You know those fellows?' Harry asked her, his face a mask of concern.

At the determined nod of her head, Ether asked, 'How about you, will they know you on sight?'

She gave her head a negative shake.

'Then you get to your room and stay out of sight,' he directed. 'We'll see what they want.'

Regina put a fearful look on the two men. 'Mr Logan?' she asked.

'Not a word about him,' Ether spoke up. 'He took most of his gear with him this morning. If he comes back tonight and the men are still here, we might get a chance to tip him off about our guests. If they are simply passing through, they'll be gone.'

'Don't care for this much,' Harry told his partner. 'You remember the army supply wagon that comes through each month? It's due any day now. I can't believe this visit is a coincidence.'

The men were at the door so Regina hurried to the back of the store and went into her room. She hurriedly began to change her clothes while listening to the conversation.

'Howdy!' Lott was the one to speak. 'Me and the boys could use a meal and a place to spend the night.'

'Where you heading?' Ether asked.

'Colorado . . . over near Denver,' Lott replied. 'We are going to help my brother with his ranch. He is one of the few who didn't lose most of his cattle to that damnable winter blizzard which roared through here last month.'

'I'd think you would be taking the train for that journey,' Harry remarked. 'The plains can be real tough this time of year. We get another storm like the last one and you'll be goners for sure.'

Lott shrugged. 'If we had the money, we'd sure enough have gone that route.' Then turning back to his original questions. 'How about it? Can we get a meal and place to put up for the night?'

Ether gave a bob of his head. 'We're pretty short on supplies, but we can rustle you up some venison stew. Far as sleeping goes, there's the barn or inside here on the floor of our eating room.'

'Much obliged,' Lott said. 'We don't have a lot of money, but we'll give you a couple dollars for your hospitality.'

Harry said, 'That's fair enough for us. We often provide food and shelter to wayfaring travelers.'

Lott paused and pointed to his men. 'This here is Delaward . . . that's Sax,' he moved his finger as he introduced them. 'And Prince . . . Ackers, and I'm Lott.'

'Ether Boyle,' Ether replied. 'My pard is Harry Beaumont.'

'All right if we put our horses in the corral?'

'There ought to be enough feed and water to take care of them for the night. We keep the team horses well fed and ready for use.'

'Not expecting any stages this evening are you?' Lott asked.

'No, nothing due in for a coupla days.'

'Then we'll see you in a few minutes and sure do thank you for your hospitality.'

As soon as the five men were outside, Regina peeked out the door. She was back to wearing her Indian clothes and had smeared a little ash from the fire pit on her face. While she didn't think Ackers would recognize her, it was better to hide her attractive features as best she could. She worked quickly to weave her hair into braids as she entered the main room.

'Good idea,' Ether said, seeing what she was up to. 'Less questions if you look like an Indian squaw who is simply helping out around the store.'

Harry added, 'To be on the cautious side, don't you be caught out of your room without me or Ether being handy.'

'Yeah, we don't want any of those men getting ideas.'

Regina couldn't hide the terror she felt at seeing Lott and Ackers again. 'I'll do as you say,' she replied.

'Might not be anything to this visit other than what they said,' Harry surmised. 'It's a full day from here to anywhere else, no matter which way they travel. It makes sense to spend the night here.'

'They are killers,' Regina stated through clenched teeth.

'We know, little lady, but we'll just have to wait it out,' Ether said. 'Five of them against us two, we wouldn't have a prayer of winning in a gunfight.'

Harry looked out the lone window. 'Let's hope Jess sees the extra horses and comes in careful like. With his help, we might be able to take them.'

Ether grunted his doubt. 'Well, until they pull something, we can only stay the trail and hope for the best.'

Prince stared at the station house, while the horses were being tended to. Lott didn't miss his intense concentration.

'What is it?'

'There was someone else in the station. I heard the rustle of clothing or something – came from that adjacent room, the one attached to the north side of the building.'

'We'll play this careful,' Lott warned the fancy-dressed gunman. 'One of us will stay outside until we find out what we're up against. We don't want any surprises.'

Prince allowed a twisted smirk to play on his lips. 'Someone comes charging out of that room with a gun and I'll send a lead greeting through his heart.'

'We don't want any gunplay, leastways until we get the payroll. If it comes to a shooting contest, we'll do whatever is necessary.'

Sax had walked over and heard the remark. 'What's that?' he queried, a frown coming into his face. 'You talking about killing them?'

Prince spun on Sax, his hand on his gun, eyes flashing with a death warning. 'You're about one breath away from being a dead man, Sax!' He snarled the words. 'Damned if I ain't sick and tired of your eavesdropping and whining!'

Sax staggered back as if he had walked into a solid right fist to the jaw. 'What?' he managed the single word in little more than a whisper.

Lott raised a hand to prevent Sax from answering, while stepping between the two men. 'Let's not do anything stupid and frighten our hosts, boys. We're all in this together and don't want them getting skittish.'

Sax recovered a bit of courage, facing Lott. 'You never said anything about killing. This is supposed to be a robbery.'

'We're only discussing what could happen if things got out of hand. Prince thinks there was someone hiding in the next room – that's what we were talking about.'

The worried expression remained on Sax's face.

'Unbutton your collar and relax, Sax,' Prince remarked easily. 'If you didn't have ears like an elephant, you wouldn't have heard us talking at all. I don't like anyone snooping over my shoulder.'

Lott forced a consoling laugh. 'There's nothing to get all nervous about, Sax. You should learn to joke around once in awhile. You're too damned serious for your own good.'

Sax attempted a smile, but it didn't hide his suspicions. 'Hey, sorry about that, Lott,' he said. 'I guess I'm just a little nervous about taking on seven troopers.'

'We all have to be on our toes to get the job done. That's why it's important we don't have any surprises from the station help.'

'Sure, Lott, I understand.'

'If we're all ready, let's head over and partake of the culinary delights awaiting us for supper.' He paused to look at Delaward. 'You hang back until we know what is in that back room.'

The man gave a nod of understanding.

Prince was all smiles again. 'Bet they serve up a

111

feast fit for a king, eh, Sax?'

Sax, feeling a little better and relieved not to have his favorite body full of fresh bullet holes, also forced a chuckle. 'Yeah, it might even beat a can of beans.'

There was no way Regina could hide out until the men chose to move on. She was visible when four of the five men entered the station. All of them looked her direction, but the fancy-dressed one was the one who troubled her most. He had eyes like a lizard, dull and vacant, other than for a glimmer of intense interest.

'Whose squaw is that?' he asked.

'She is a Sioux Indian,' Ether explained. 'The rest of the group she was with died in an avalanche during the blizzard. She made her way here and is working for her keep.'

'Pretty thing,' Prince observed, 'if you were to clean her up some.'

'She doesn't speak any English, but she understands sign pretty well,' Harry told the group. 'She isn't much of a cook, but you know what Indians eat. We're trying to teach her something about white man's meals.'

'She the only other one here?' Lott asked, looking over at the door to the attached room.'

'Yep, my nephew used to help out but he moved on. We had the extra room so we took her in.'

112

Lott said, 'Good thing or she would have sure enough died out there in this icy cold weather.'

No one said anything for a moment; the tension hung in the air. It was like having a surly bear lumber into the room and no one daring to mention it. Lott suspected these two old-timers recognized they were up to mischief, but they didn't have any choice but to play out the hand.

As for Lott and his boys, figuring the pair knew they were in for trouble, it was only a matter of time until trouble started. It was a game of chess where the next move could win or lose the game, yet neither side dared make that first move.

Delaward entered the building to break the strained quietude. 'There's a breeze coming up. Going to be frosty once the sun sets. I—' He stopped in mid-sentence, spotting the girl. 'Well, say! Where'd the pretty little Indian maid come from? I ain't seen one as cute as her since I was at the fort over near the Platt River. They had a bunch of Cheyenne women and children come in to keep from freezing during the blizzard.' He displayed a lecherous sneer. 'Trouble with the fort commander, he didn't allow for no fraternizing.'

'Her family died from an avalanche,' Ackers filled him in on the girl. 'She is earning her keep with the two station owners.'

'Hope she can cook,' Delaward said. Another

leering smirk, 'Else she'll have to find some other means to earn her way.'

Ether turned to Regina and gave her a couple hand signals. She hurried into the kitchen to begin filling plates for the men.

'Sit yourselves down at the table,' Harry offered. 'I've got some cider to go with the meal. We weren't planning on any guests tonight, so you'll have to make do with leftover stew and cider.'

'It beats trying to find enough dry kindling to get a fire going and try to cook out in this snow,' Lott said. 'It'll do just fine.'

Prince caught a sharp glance from Ackers and went to the door. 'I forgot to check my horse's front foot. He was favoring it before we stopped. I'd best get a look while it's still light enough to see.'

'We'll save you a plate of stew,' Lott told him.

Harry and Ether also exchanged looks. It did not escape their attention that Prince left as Delaward entered. The five men were being careful, always having one of their number moving about. That way they kept a constant lookout for anyone else coming, and it would be difficult to get the drop on all of them at once. It was obvious Lott and his men were expecting trouble. The problem for Ether and Harry, there was little they could do against five wary gunmen.

114

CHAPTER NINE

The snow had filled in the lower hollows and ravines forcing Jess and his animals to buck through five- and six-foot drifts. By the time he reached the range of mountains, it was early afternoon. Then it was close to impossible to sneak up on any game. Only topping a hill in time to see several deer making their way out of the next valley allowed him a shot.

For a time during the war the Confederates had used sharpshooters to slow down the Yankee forces. A couple snipers could halt a patrol or even a company of men with a few well-aimed shots. Jess had been among those men chosen to do the long-range shooting and was a good shot. What money he could put together after the war was used to buy himself a Winchester Model 1866, a lever-action .44 carbine that was head and shoulders above the old single-shot muzzle-loading .50 caliber he had used in the war.

He had only a few seconds before the deer were out of both range and sight, but his gun was ready for use. Dismounting from Champ, he secured the reins to an exposed sagebrush, moved a few steps away and took careful aim. Employing his learned method of distance reckoning, he lifted the gun slightly above the target to allow for the approximate five hundred yards and led the biggest buck in the group by a few feet. He knew he would get only one shot.

He made it count.

The buck jumped with surprise as the gunshot echoed through the still air. He was not knocked off of his feet by the bullet but stumbled several steps and then darted away from the group. A couple of the deer started to follow in his direction, but then fell back with the others and were soon out of sight over the hill.

Jess climbed aboard Champ, but took his time. He knew how a wounded deer behaved. It would run till it dropped if it heard or sensed anyone on its back trail. If the animal ran a short way and detected no one chasing or following, it would often lie down. Once down, a severely wounded deer would not be able to get up again. It usually saved time to let the deer feel safe enough to bed down and lick its wound.

Allowing the buck a full thirty minutes, Jess picked up a blood trail and found the deer after another quarter mile. He had settled beneath a patch of scrub brush and had died there.

He dressed out the animal as the sun hung low in the eastern sky. It was going to be late before he made it back to the station, but he decided traveling in the dark would beat finding a sheltered cove or using his poncho to make a lean-to for the night. He strapped the deer on the mule and bundled up for the cold ride.

He ate the last of his hard rolls as he rode, watching the sun disappear over the horizon. It would be dark soon, but he was almost out of the foothills. Once he reached the flatlands, he would pick up and follow his own trail. That would help him find his way until the moon put in an appearance.

Allowing Champ to set his own pace, Jess let his mind wander. It didn't travel far before it conjured up Regina. He could only imagine how hard life had been for her – carrying the label of bad luck all these years. The tribe had obviously treated her like an outsider, because of a couple accidents and the deaths of two suitors. They even blamed the avalanche on her!

He closed his eyes for a moment and pictured her after the rescue, once they were back at the trading post. While the place was crowded with twenty Indian men, women and children, he had caught sight of her on occasion. She had continually shown concern for the children and he had not said a word to her

117

until they were filing out of the cabin. She had given him an odd look when he had spoken to her, one of curiosity and a measure of comprehension. Next he envisioned her quiet beauty after she had been a gift to him. She had made sign that she wanted to go with him, then later she refused to get on the back of his horse. The images flashed through his mind's eye and moved forward to when she had attacked a strange man for no apparent reason. After being locked in the jail cell, she appeared fearful he was leaving her to fend for herself. A warmth crept into his chest at the memory of the hug she had given him for getting her out. He continued to ride and went on with his imaginings to when he had provided her with a bath. She had been both puzzled and grateful, then stubborn about not wearing the dress to bed. And finally, she had come to him before he left, stood within his embrace like a wife, kissing him and saying goodbye to her husband. It caused his chest to swell with an unfamiliar pride or satisfaction.

A smile played along his lips at the memories, while a yearning heated him from the inside, a desire to have her be more than a companion or slave. She had shown him a mature side, qualities of a real woman, and he liked it.

Darkness covered the land, but the whiteness of the snow outlined the darker tracks his animals had made on the trek into the hills. He remembered there had been a near full moon the previous night. Once it rose into the sky, he would be able to find his way back without any trouble.

Regina felt the eyes of the gunmen on her. Prince and Delaward were the worst, leering after her as if they could remove her clothing with hungry looks. She found herself moving about self-consciously, concerned she would inhale too deeply when standing upright, or she would have to reach over the table or bend in such a way the man would see the contours of her form. She avoided Ackers and Lott completely, afraid she might give away the deep-seated hatred that churned inside of her like fiery embers.

As she worked, she wondered what would happen when Jess arrived. If he simply rode in, the gang of killers would have him trapped and controlled, the same as they had her and the two station employees. Although no one had said anything yet, she knew the three of them were prisoners. If only she had a window in her room, she would have escaped into the night and found a way to warn him.

Once the meal was served and the men fed, she cleaned up the dirty dishes and put them away for morning. Ether pointed out that there was adequate salt pork and grits for breakfast. He also gave her a consoling look and whispered that everything would be all right. There was little conviction in his voice and she knew he feared they might all be killed the following day.

She finished her duties and started for her room when Delaward caught hold of her wrist. He was sitting at the long table and attempted to pull her down on to his lap. With her still being on her feet, however, she had the advantage. She offered no resistance, until she was turned in the same direction as bench and table. Then she put a hand against his chest and gave a mighty shove!

Delaward had been sitting at the end of the table and the bench offered no support for his back. He let go of her and fell off the bench backwards. She scurried away as Lott and Ackers laughed at the man's clumsy attempt.

'She's too quick for you,' Lott laughed. 'You want to catch a wild filly, you'd best get yourself a long rope.'

Ackers also heckled the man. 'Yeah, and you have to be sure and set the noose first, before you try and reel in an unbroken mustang.'

Regina did not linger. She hurried into her room and shut the door. There was no lock, but it closed from the inside so she slid the dressing table over to block anyone from entering. Then placing her ear to the wall, she listened to the men still teasing

Delaward. After a few tense moments, she allowed herself a sigh of relief. No one had followed after her.

Prince was the loudest talker of the group. He proclaimed that Delaward didn't know how to handle women, but that he would show him one day soon.

The fifth man, Sax, was outside somewhere. They were not so blatant as to admit they had a man on constant watch, but one of them was always out in the darkness. It made it impossible to find a way to warn Jess. He was bound to ride in and be caught along with her, Harry and Ether.

Tears burned at the backs of her eyes. She hadn't cried in many years, but the thought of Jess being killed was worse than the idea of dying herself. She searched the room for a weapon, but the only thing she could find was a small broken branch mixed in with the firewood. It was only good for use as a short club, but she would keep it handy in case she got a chance to use it.

Jess was a short distance from the way station when he spied the light from the solitary front window. He started to speed up, thinking someone must have waited up for him, but then he caught sight of the corral and several extra horses. He pulled Champ and his packmule to a stop and studied the yard for a long moment. His caution was rewarded when he spied the glowing tip of a cigarette, belonging to a man standing just inside the barn door. What was he doing outside in this bitter cold? Was he waiting for someone?

Something was definitely amiss.

Instead of approaching the yard, he moved off the trail to a stand of buck brush and tethered his two animals. Then he skirted along the ridge of the hill and crept down to the back of the barn. Using both stealth and the darkness, he eased inside through the rear door and sneaked his way to where he could see the man. He seemed preoccupied and didn't hear his quiet approach. Edging up to within ten feet, Jess stopped and pointed his gun at the man's back.

'Sing out and I'll plug you like a practice tin can,' he said icily.

The man froze in position, though he did drop the cigarette.

'Keep your back to me and toss your shooting iron,' Jess ordered.

Offering no resistance the man crushed the smoke under his heel and did as he was told.

Quickly moving up next to the man, Jess checked him for other weapons; he never offered a bit of resistance.

'Now who are you and what's going on?' Jess asked, pressing the muzzle of his gun up against the man's ear. 'Lie to me, and it'll be the last thing you ever do.'

'My name is Sax and I'm supposed to keep watch for any strangers' – he uttered a grunt of defeat – 'like you for instance.'

'How many of you are there and why are you here?'

'I hired on with a couple men a short while back . . . named Lott and Ackers, to do a job. There's two more with them inside, a hard case named Delaward and a dude who talks like a big man with a gun.'

'You're here to do a job?' he repeated. 'What kind of job? A robbery of some kind, a payroll or strong box from a stage?'

The man's shoulders slumped in defeat. 'Listen, mister, I got down on my luck and throwed in with these guys. It was supposed to be a simple hold-up, but I'm afraid they might end up killing some of those soldiers. I didn't sign on to get involved in no killings.'

'Soldiers . . . an army payroll?'

'The supply wagon is due in here tomorrow. First off I was told we were going to take them by surprise and lock them in a shed or something. Since then I overheard some other talk and it sounded like they might shoot some of them.' He sighed. 'I didn't know what to do. I've been standing here thinking I ought to saddle my horse and ride out. I would have already, but I feared they would hear me and run me down. I don't want to die.'

'What about the people who live and work here?' he asked.

'I don't know about the two old men, but both Delaward and the dude have ideas about an Indian girl who is staying here. Don't know where that is going to lead, but I don't want any part of it.'

Jess backed up and had the man turn around. It was dark, but he had good night vision and, with the moon bright against the nearby snow covered ground, he could see the man's face clearly. 'If you could get away clean, what would you do?'

'The troopers are at Granville. I'd ride that way and warn them.' He shrugged. 'After that, I'd head for the nearest big city and not look back. I can work a faro table, stock grocery shelves, even ride herd on cattle till I get my life back in order. This was the dumbest mistake of my life . . . I mean that.'

'How can I know you're telling me the truth?'

'As God is my judge, I've never harmed another person – 'less you count during the war. This is the first time I ever thought about robbing anyone and it's because I was drinking with Delaward when the job offer came along. It sounded like easy money and a way to start a new life. I reckon I'd have been riding with a heavy guilt the rest of my life for stealing the money . . . even if it was from a bunch of ex-Yanks.'

'You fought for the South?'

'Kansas Southern Volunteers under Colonel

Bonneville. Lost two cousins at Gettysburg and carry the scar from a bit of shrapnel in my side. An inch to the right and I wouldn't be wondering about my future.'

'I served with some Texas volunteers right up until Lee surrendered,' Jess told him. 'Still don't cotton to Yanks, but I sure wouldn't kill a bunch of them for money.'

'Me neither. I didn't know about the possibility of killing until it was too late to back out. Makes me downright sick to think on it.'

'If I let you go, you have to promise to tell the soldiers there is a trap waiting for them.' Jess leveled the gun at the man's chest. 'Swear it on the lives of all those who fell in battle fighting for the Confederacy . . . including your cousins.'

'You got my word on it,' Sax vowed. 'I'll ride all night and meet up with them boys before they leave town. They'll come here ready for trouble – I promise you that.'

Jess holstered his gun, feeling certain he could trust the man.

'When do you get relieved?'

'Delaward is supposed to come out at midnight. What's that, maybe a coupla hours or so?'

'About that,' Jess said, pulling out his timepiece long enough to check. 'Yeah, we've got a little over two hours. Pick up your gear and get your horse saddled while I take care of my animals. I'll come in the back and you can take your horse out that way. If you stick to the side of the hill until you reach the roadway, no one will see you, even if they happen to look out the window.'

Ten minutes later Sax was ready to leave and Jess was working on how he could deal with the remaining gunmen.

'Good of you to trust me,' Sax said, holding out his hand. 'I thank you for giving me a chance to make this whole thing right. I'd have hated myself for the rest of my life if I'd have helped kill a couple innocent people – even Yanks.' After a quick handshake, 'You be careful with these gents, they are as deadly as any you'll ever come across.'

Jess said, 'I'll do what I can here. If I get lucky, I might be able to enter the house and catch them sleeping.'

'They have been real cautious to this point,' Sax warned. 'Don't stick your neck out too far. Once I warn the troopers, you'll have plenty of help.'

'I won't risk getting caught. You go ahead and get started.'

Sax turned up the collar to his coat and tugged his hat down to cover his ears. It was going to be a cold ride. Then the would-be robber took hold of his horse. 'Luck to you, friend.'

'In case I don't get the chance to corral these mavericks, tell whoever is in charge of the troopers that I'll try to get the civilians out of harm's way.'

'And who're you, so's I can tell the blue-bellies the name of the Reb who is on their side?'

'Jess Logan.'

He arched his brows in surprise. 'Jess Logan . . . the bounty hunter?'

Jess groaned. 'Don't tell me you've heard of me?'

'Prince – the dude who thinks he's a gunfighter – he's inside the station. He thinks you're after him.'

'I was following him for a time, but didn't think I'd ever catch up to him.'

'Well, you done caught up to him, but he ain't alone.'

'With your help and those soldier boys we'll take care of him and all of his pals.'

'You can count on me,' Sax vowed. Then he turned and led his horse out the back way. He was gone within moments.

Well, Logan, Jess muttered to himself, *you sure know when to hire on to a new job. Goldurned if you don't!*

CHAPTER TEN

Jess strung the deer up in a tree and hoped nothing could reach it. Once the horses were tethered in a nearby cove, he began to turn over ideas for dealing with the four bandits. He thought the best strategy was to take Delaward out of the fight and then slip inside pretending to be Sax. If the others were all asleep, and with the help of Ether and Harry, they could get the drop on them and then wait for the cavalry to arrive. That *was* the plan . . . until two men came out of the building.

Jess held his breath and backed into the darkest shadows, staying out of sight of the two approaching men.

'Sonuva Buck, it's cold out here!' one man complained.

'This makes sense though, Prince,' the other said. 'Three inside and two out, just in case those old codgers try something. No way they will mess with us while we're split up this way. We were too wide open with just one man out here.'

'Lot of worry for nothing, I say. We could have locked those three in a room and been sleeping peaceful all night.'

'Delaward, you're a man after my own heart . . . except I was thinking we should just shoot them and be done with it.'

'Even the girl?'

Prince laughed. 'Not right away. She's got more worth than those two old men.'

'Reckon Lott knows what he's doing,' Delaward said. 'Something goes wrong and a stage or some other visitors show up before the supply wagon, we'll need the station hands to make things look natural.'

'Might even need them for hostages, should we find ourselves trapped too,' Prince agreed. 'Guess we'll just have to spend the night on watch and try not to freeze.'

'What say, Sax?' Delaward asked loudly, a step from the doorway. 'You ready for some sack time?'

Jess vanished back into the darkness and quietly padded to the back door. It was ajar from Sax's exit, so that worked to his advantage. He was quickly out into the snow, but kept next to the building so he could overhear the two men.

'Where you at, Sax?' Prince sounded miffed. 'I

find you asleep and I'll put a slug through your teeth!'

'Damn!' Jess heard Delaward snarl. 'His horse is gone!' After a short silence, 'And his tack is missing.'

'That whiny yellow dog turned tail and took off!' Prince declared. 'I knew we couldn't trust that coward to stick. Soon as he heard we might have to do some shooting he sneaks off without a word.'

'Reckon he knew if he opened his mouth, one of us would have shut it . . . for good.'

'What do we do about it?' Prince wondered. 'I don't see how waking up Ackers and Lott would do any good. It's not like we can go after him. He probably left as soon as it was dark. I'll bet he has a three or four hour head start.'

'You're right about that. And I'm not about to saddle up and try and follow him in the dark.'

'You think he might squeal to someone about our plan?' Prince asked.

'No, he's too much of a weasel. I'd guess he'll run to the nearest hole and bury himself for about a week. He can't be sure them soldier boys could take us, even if they were alerted to a trap.'

'And if they didn't get us all. . . .' Prince let the words hang. The obvious answer was that whoever was left would seek him out and kill him for being a rat. Delaward uttered a grunt of agreement and the two fell silent.

Jess was forced to set his foot down very gently on to his own tracks to keep from making any more noise than necessary. With the horses milling about, stirring because of the arrival of the two noisy men, his retreating footsteps went undetected.

He headed toward his horse and the packmule. He would picket them further back in the hills and out of sight. Then he would bed down for the night and try to figure a plan. The one thing in his favor was Sax. The soldiers would come into Lakota Crossing prepared. All he had to do was give them the nod when they arrived, so they would know he was the one on their side.

Sax reached Granville shortly after daybreak. No one was on the street or moving about yet, so he went over to the jail. If the soldiers were in town, the marshal would know about it.

A voice growled about being rousted out of bed but answered the door after the second knock.

'Sorry to bother you, Marshal,' Sax apologized, shivering from the cold. 'I wonder if you could tell me if a small troop of soldiers has arrived yet – they were traveling with a supply wagon. I need to talk to the man in charge.'

'I had a drink with Lieutenant Goldman over at the saloon last night. They were going to get an early start.' The marshal paused to look out to see the sun was not yet up. 'You'll likely find a couple of them putting their team in harness over at the Widow Noonan's. Her husband was a retired colonel, so she made room for the army boys in her house. She has a large corral in the back.' He pointed, 'Down at the end of the street and turn left. It's the house sitting back off the road.'

'Thanks, Marshal,' Sax said. 'Again, I'm sorry to have woken you up.'

'Yeah, well who else you gonna ask directions from . . . ain't no one else stirring this early.'

Sax flinched at the cynical tone of voice, but the lawman raised a hand in farewell and closed the door. Sax climbed back on his horse and found the Noonan house a short way from town. Indeed, he spied a man out harnessing the horses, so he headed for him at a quick pace. The sooner he put this behind him the better.

The man hitching up the horses had two stripes on his sleeve. He stopped at Sax's approach and regarded him with a curious look on his face.

'That's close enough.' He stopped Sax a few feet away. 'State your business, mister.'

Sax halted his horse and looked around for more soldiers. Evidently this man was working alone. It gave him some assurance to see that he was not a mere private.

'I know you're moving more than supplies,' he

132

began. 'And I've come to give your commander a warning.'

His statement provoked the man's interest. 'Not supplies,' he repeated. 'And how would you know what we are or are not carrying, mister?'

'That's not important at the moment. Where is your commanding officer?'

'I'm Corporal Felding. You tell me what is important and I'll decide if I want to interrupt my lieutenant's breakfast.'

'There are several men waiting to ambush you at Lakota Crossing.'

The corporal's eyes widened in surprise. 'Ambush? There's an ambush waiting for us?'

'Yes.'

His expression grew serious . . . and suspicious. 'How do you know about this ambush?'

'I just came from there,' Sax replied. 'I rode all night to get here in time to warn you. They have taken over the way station and will be waiting for you.'

Corporal Felding seemed to make up his mind. 'Best climb down from your horse and I'll take you in to see the lieutenant.'

Sax stiffly swung his right leg over the saddle and stepped down. His left foot came out of the stirrup and touched ground . . . just as a knife sank deeply in between his ribs!

Sax gasped from the sudden excruciating pain! He opened his mouth to cry out, but a second plunge of the knife went in far enough to puncture his lung. His wind was lost like a suddenly deflated balloon. Without air, no words escaped his lips.

Felding moved up against him, holding him up, his left hand placed beneath Sax's right shoulder. His third thrust of the blade was the last bit of pain Sax knew. Then there was nothing but blackness.

Lott kept up the ploy of being ordinary men traveling the next morning. He told Ether and Harry that Sax had gone out to do some hunting. They were hoping he could bag enough meat to tide them over for a couple more days on the trail. It made an excuse for their missing man and allowed them to stay one more day to rest the other animals.

Ether and Harry pretended to be taken in, but they were puzzled about the disappearance of one of the men. Soon as breakfast was over, the waystation men and Regina managed to be alone for a few minutes.

'Something ain't right,' Ether said in a hushed voice. 'That Sax fellow looked about the least like a bandit of the bunch.'

'Could be that he's the best hunter though,' Harry suggested. 'And they might need the meat if they are on the run.' He grunted. 'Either that or he's keeping

134

watch up the trail for what they are really after.'

'They are all bad men,' Regina said firmly. 'Lott and Ackers have robbed and killed for many years.'

Harry eyed her closely. 'Let me go out on a limb here – one of those men is the one you attacked in Granville.' Regina blinked in surprise and he went on. 'I saw the one named Ackers has a bruised ear and some swelling on the side of his head.'

'Yes,' she admitted. 'He and Lott killed my family.'

'You surely do speak better English than most Indians,' Ether observed. 'Where did you learn again?'

'No time for small talk,' Harry said. 'We have to think up a plan.'

'What can we do against four of them?' Ether asked.

'We must warn Mr Logan,' Regina said.

'He's a smart guy,' Harry told her. 'He'll likely spot them or their horses before he shows himself. We only have to be ready when and if he starts something.'

'With him in the mix, it would be three against four . . . but they are gun hands and neither of us can shoot for shucks.'

'Question is, what do they intend to do with us?' Harry wondered.

'There won't be much of value on one of the stages . . . unless a business or bank is moving some money.' Ether frowned in thought. 'That only leaves the army supply wagon. It's due anytime.'

'And they might be carrying a payroll for the nearby forts. That would be a sizable amount.'

'Makes sense, Harry. And it would explain why there are five men. The supply wagon usually has five or six riders and a driver.'

Before any of them could speak again, Prince came into the room. He flashed a leering smirk at Regina.

'You fellows still having a time getting our cook to fix white man's food?'

'She's catching on,' Ether replied. 'Takes a little effort to get past the language barrier, but we're getting there.'

Prince barely flicked his eyes to Ether before speaking again. 'Looks as if we're sticking around today so the horses can rest up.' Again studying Regina, 'I'm not much for eating first thing in the morning. What's for lunch?'

'We've got some beans and a little leftover pork. We were just trying to explain to Pale Flower about how to make cornbread.'

'Beans and ham with cornbread . . . sounds good.' He didn't offer to leave, but pulled up a stool and sat down. 'Anything I can do to help move things along?'

'Might bring in an armload of wood from around

back,' Harry suggested.

'I'll send Delaward. He needs the exercise.'

Ether could see they were not going to have the room to themselves. He said he would start making out the next freight order for food and supplies and entered the main room. Harry didn't want to leave Pale Flower alone with the killer, so he began to demonstrate how to make cornbread. Although the words were unspoken, it was clear the gang was going to keep a close watch on them. That meant they weren't going to be allowed enough privacy to plan a move against them. They could only hope Jess spotted the gang before he rode in and was taken captive too.

The liveryman was out of breath when he found Marshal Renny at Etta Mae's and hurried over to his table.

'Found a body just now – hidden in a pile of used straw – right there at the stable!' the man blurted out. 'Deader 'n your boots he is, with stab wounds in the chest.'

Renny stood up. He would be leaving the rest of the meal. It had been written on the blackboard which listed the daily special as the Rustlers' Breakfast. He knew he wasn't going to miss much, because them there rustlers had sure enough stolen all of the meat from the breakfast special. It was nothing more than fried mush, rock-hard biscuits and burnt toast.

'Show me,' he told the hostler, following him out of the eating emporium.

Arriving moments later, Renny recognized the body at once. 'This man asked me for directions to the army supply wagon. I wonder how he ended up like this?'

'I saw a saddled horse in the corral and found him after looking around,' the liveryman explained. 'I figured a customer had come in late and was sleeping in the loft or something. Then I saw a toe sticking out of the dirty straw pile.'

Renny did a quick examination. 'Yep, stabbed two or three times. He likely died without making a sound.'

'Who could have put him here?'

Renny looked around and spotted some deep-imprinted tracks from a man's boot. 'Looks like a man carrying a heavy load,' he told the hostler. 'See there . . . how the return tracks are not as deep. The man carried the body here to hide it.'

Going to the door of the barn he saw the direction of the prints. 'Came from over at the Widow Noonan's place. This gent was killed by one of the soldiers.'

'Why would one of them soldier boys kill him?'

Renny frowned, the same thought going through

his own mind. He scanned the dead man's face and remembered him from a couple days back. He and four others had been over at the saloon. Funny how he had arrived back in town alone. And why did he want to find the lieutenant and talk to him?

'There's something in the wind that don't smell good,' he told the hostler. 'Saddle my bronc while I get my heavy coat and traveling gear. I'll be back in ten minutes.'

'I'll have your hoss ready,' the man promised.

CHAPTER ELEVEN

Hours passed and Jess kept watch over the station from a lone stand of scrub brush. It wasn't a good place to be discovered as there was no cover to either side. However, if anyone did any talking out in the yard, he might overhear some of the words and it was close enough to get a look inside the station when the door was open. The problem with such a location was that the only move he could make unseen would be to back away until he could slip over the hill. From there he could stay below the horizon and come up wherever he wanted along the ridge overlooking the corral.

Sax leaving in the night had put the killers on alert. No one came or went from the house alone. Jess didn't know whether that was fear Sax might tell someone about the ambush or if it was to keep Ether

140

and Harry from attempting any action against them.

For a time, he wondered if he shouldn't go up the trail and meet with the soldiers. He had put himself in a box that was open only to the front. With the rugged hills back of him, there was too much snow for his horse to ford some of the drifts. And to go on foot might put him a mile from his horse and the crossing about the time the army arrived. He felt the best plan was to keep watch and stay ready. When the troopers arrived, he might be of some help, but he would need to make certain they knew he was on their side. It would be a sad end to get killed by the very men he was trying to help.

By late afternoon, there was a hollow feeling in Jess's stomach for want of something to eat. He had finished the last of the hard rolls and was down to using snow for water. His two animals were no better off, gnawing at the few strips of bark on the scrub brush, nibbling whatever they could find. If the army wagon didn't arrive today, he would have to cut enough venison from the deer for his supper. That would mean starting a fire and that would be as risky as—

Ether and Harry suddenly came out of the station, followed at once by Regina. Two men trailed back of them with guns. The three were herded to the storage shed . . . the one full of harnesses and wagon parts. It had a lock on the door and no windows, a perfect cell for holding prisoners. He would get no help from Ether or Harry, but at least they and Regina would be out of harm's way.

Jess watched as the three were locked inside and then the men scurried around to get into position. Even as he looked further up the trail he spied the wagon and outriders. An instant alarm shot through him. The troopers were riding with two in front, four behind and the driver on the wagon. Not a one of them even had their carbine out for use. Unless there were men hiding inside the covered wagon, they were riding directly into the trap unawares.

At the bend in the trail, Jess could see into the covered wagon and through the open back flaps. No men were visible except for the driver. Sax hadn't warned them; he had lied to Jess!

An instant panic set in. Jess lifted his gun, but the four men were well concealed. With the eyes of the four gunmen on the troopers, he could move in a little closer, but the hillside offered no place for cover. If he opened fire to warn the troopers, he would be exposed on both sides and likely be killed in short order. Besides which, the wagon was only a short distance away. The men were already close enough to be cut down by the bandits. To fire a warning shot might cause the death of all the troopers. He didn't want to be responsible for the lives of seven soldiers . . . even if they were all ex-Yanks. Jess held his fire and watched, praying no one would be hurt.

The troopers entered the yard and one held up a hand to stop the procession. The action prompted an immediate response. Four gunmen showed themselves, guns drawn and aimed at the soldiers. Two of them were yelling for the troopers to raise their hands.

One soldier grabbed for his gun and two shots rang out, knocking him and another out of their saddles. The mounted soldiers milled about for a moment, but they had no chance. The man in charge called out for calm and the troopers raised their hands.

One of the bandits who hadn't fired his gun climbed up on to the wagon. The driver made a grab for his gun, but the bandit was too quick for him. He brutally clubbed the driver alongside the head. The driver slumped forward and the robber hit him a second time to make sure he would pose no further threat.

Jess groaned, helpless, and stared hard at the two soldiers lying on the ground. Neither of them moved. The killers were very accurate with their guns. Two men dead, the driver beaten unconscious and maybe dying, and the final four troopers had surrendered their weapons. With the station help

already locked away, the plan was working to per-
fection and he had done nothing to stop it. If only
he hadn't trusted Sax. He should have made his
move during the night. He might have managed to
disarm the four killers and have them safely locked
in the shed. Instead, he'd sat by while two or three
men had been killed and the others were out of the
fight.

Quite suddenly a thought entered his head. He
still had his sniper's skill to fall back on. If he could
bring down the odds, there still might be a chance to
prevent the robbery and the death of any more soldiers.

Jess moved carefully and retreated to the top of
the hill. Once out of sight, he moved to a point
where he could take up a position and see the yard
below. A knobby windswept knoll protected him,
although it was a fairly long way for a shot. Guessing
the distance at two hundred yards, he reasoned it was
not near as hard as shooting the buck the previous
day.

He didn't know which gunman was which, but he
had seen the two who killed the troopers. It was time
to cut the odds. Then he would see if his luck would
hold long enough to bluff the remaining bandits
into giving up.

The soldiers were gathered into a group, except
for the unconscious driver on the wagon, who hadn't

144

twitched since being clubbed. Jess decided it would be smart to let the men be locked away. He could better protect them once they were all together in the sturdy shed.

He used the few moments to warm his hands and get his Winchester ready. One of the men who had shot and killed a soldier escorted the troopers to the shed. Jess sighted down the rifle and mentally judged the windage and elevation. As the man closed the door and locked it, his back was turned to Jess. It offered a wide target and he squeezed the trigger.

His aim was true. The bullet dropped the man flat before he realized he'd been hit. Not watching him, Jess swung his gun around. It was too late to fire a second shot as the bandits all scrambled to take cover behind the wagon.

'Who the hell is that?' one cried out to the others.

'Can't be Sax,' growled another voice. 'He ain't got the sand to come back and take us on.'

'Filthy bushwhacker kilt Delaward!' a third shouted. 'I can see his eyes are wide open and he's got a mouthful of dirt.'

Jess didn't want to give them time to think. They might get creative and figure a way to get to use their hostages, so he called out to them.

'You three bandits down there!' he hollered, keeping the gun ready for instant use. 'This is Jess Logan! I'm the bounty hunter who took in Bloody

Bill Gates and I've come for the one who calls himself Prince.' He let the words hang, knowing the three men would be trying to find a way to fire back at him. However, they only had pistols and he had a rifle. He was uphill too. It gave him a sizable advantage in any exchange of gunfire.

'We've got a half-dozen people locked in the shed down here,' one of them yelled back. 'You start shooting again and some of them are going to die.'

'That looks to be a slab-built storage shed. I'd wager it's full of harness gear, single-trees, wagon wheels and parts. I'm betting you could shoot at that shack for an hour with a pistol and never hit anyone inside.' He let them think about that for a few seconds. 'Besides which,' Jess continued, trying to sound as callous as possible. 'Them soldier boys ain't friends nor relatives of mine.'

The man tried a second time. 'You can't be sure a bullet won't go through the walls, and there's a girl and the two men who run this here station in there!'

'Don't know them from Adam either,' Jess barked the words. 'I'm only interested in one thing, taking in Prince for the bounty on his head. Dead or alive – his choice!'

Down at the wagon, Ackers and Lott were huddled at its rear while Prince was using the front wheel for cover. They had guns drawn but it would be next to impossible to hit Jess by shooting up the hill.

The men were involved in a discussion. It took only a short time before the voices were raised and there came an argument. Then they suddenly grew quiet.

Jess had the rifle aimed at the wagon when two guns opened up at him – one from the back of the vehicle and the other at the front – both blasting away with rapid fire. The third man suddenly darted toward the barn. He got about three steps before Jess found him in his sights. Ignoring the bullets that never even reached his position, he aimed below the waist and squeezed off a round. The bullet hit the man in mid-thigh and he sprawled headfirst on the ground. Rather than continuing to aim at him, Jess jacked another round into his rifle in case the other two had another trick up their sleeve.

The wounded man writhed in pain, clutching his wounded upper leg with both hands. He was wearing regular clothes and a worn winter hat so Jess knew he wasn't Prince. The outlaw had a reputation for dressing like a fancy dude.

'I can kill him or you can surrender to me, Prince. What's it going to be?'

There was an oath and some swearing. Then one man herded the other out into the open, his gun trained on him with each step.

'This is Prince,' the one with the gun called out. 'My name is Wayland Lott and you just shot my pard,

147

Saul Ackers. You put your gun on Prince here and let me tend to my friend.'

'No, I don't think so,' Jess said in reply. 'All three of you toss your guns out in the open; then I'll come down. I don't aim to get a bullet in my back while I'm taking custody of Prince.'

The men did as he ordered, each tossing his gun out into the middle of the yard. Jess kept his rifle pointed in their direction and started down the hill.

'I'm going to help Ackers,' Lott said. 'You've got my gun.'

'Go ahead,' Jess allowed. 'Prince, you rotate around and keep your back to me. If anyone tries something cute I'll kill you first.'

Prince pivoted about, his hands lifted high and lamented, 'You got us, all right? We're done.'

Jess was feeling pretty good about the situation. He only had to ease over and unlock the shed. Once he had the help of the troopers along with Ether and Harry, this fracas was over. But first, he would make sure Prince didn't have a second gun stored away.

He flicked a glance at the two other men. Lott was preoccupied with trying to stop the bleeding from Acker's wound. Neither appeared menacing so he concentrated on Prince. He was a dangerous man and there was likely a gallows waiting for him. He had nothing to loose by trying something.

Even as he walked past the team of horses, he

sensed movement in the wagon. The driver was stirring – he hadn't been killed.

'That's far enough, Bounty Man,' the driver's voice snarled. 'You done brought in your last man!'

CHAPTER TWELVE

Jess froze in position. A peek over his shoulder told him the driver was unhurt. He had faked being knocked out and was on his feet. His pistol was pointed at Jess and the blood running through his veins turned to ice. He was in real trouble. With his back to the man, he would have to spin and fire, in order to shoot at him. All the driver had to do was pull the trigger.

Prince rotated around and snickered in triumph. He had a second gun tucked in his waistband and a deadly malice was etched into his face.

'So you're the famous hero, the man who brought in Bloody Bill Gates,' he jeered. 'How's it feel to know you're taking your last breath, manhunter?'

'I've had better feelings,' Jess muttered, awaiting the bullet that would end his life.

'Kill him, Felding,' Prince ordered. 'I want to

watch him die.'

A gunshot rang out and Jess flinched, certain the bullet had been meant for him. Instead, he glimpsed the driver buckle at the knees and slump down on to the wagon seat. The shooter had been a man who had sneaked along the roadway until he was not a hundred feet away . . . Marshal Renny!

Prince clawed for his gun, while Jess's brain screamed at his body to react.

He whipped the rifle up and fired in a single motion, stung simultaneously by a bullet from Prince's gun. It tore a path across the bicep of his left arm and knocked the rifle from his hands.

Renny was too far away to help with Prince, but he had Lott and Ackers in his sights. The remaining live-or-die gunfight was a death match between Jess and Prince.

The fancy gunman had been hit by Jess's single shot, but it only stung him with a crease below the ribs. As Jess drew his pistol, the man quickly pulled the trigger again. Jess ignored the smoke, fire and lead. It was like being back on the Confederate lines, hearing the whine of shrapnel and whistle of cannon balls going past your head. If a man wanted to survive a heated battle, he learned to ignore everything but finding and hitting his next target.

While Prince had killed several men, most had been shot in the back or were not very skilled with a handgun. The bandit had heard the reputation of Jess Logan and hurried his shots out of desperation, firing rapidly and wildly. He missed Jess with three shots at less than forty feet.

Jess eyed only his target and squeezed off the round. It impacted the man's shirt pocket, striking him in the left side of the chest, the shot as sure and true as if Prince had been a Yank charging at him from across the battlefield. The man's face flashed into a twisted mask of shock and horror, knowing he had been killed. He toppled forward, dead before his head bounced off the snowy ground.

Renny jogged over until he was even with the wagon. He was puffing hard from the run, but took a moment to check and disarm the driver. The conspirator groaned and cursed his misfortune, doubled over from the pain of a wound in his right shoulder. As for Lott and Ackers, they had both sat out the fight and simply watched.

'Can't tell you how good it is to see you again, Marshal,' Jess said, his voice more steady than his legs. He was trembling from the fight, yet consumed with the raw energy that flooded a man's body when fighting for his very life.

'Looks like I arrived in the nick of time, Logan. Pretty careless of you not to keep an eye on the driver.'

'I saw Ackers beat him unconscious, but it was an

act . . . probably for the benefit of the lieutenant.'

'And you fell for it,' Renny teased.

'Like a sap,' Jess admitted, 'and that's a lesson I won't soon forget.'

'Where is everyone else?' he asked.

'I'll let them out, if you'll keep an eye on these three coyotes.' At Renny's nod, Jess went over and let the soldiers and others out of the shed. He was pleasantly surprised that Regina came right into his arms.

'You've been hurt!' she exclaimed, pulling back at once. 'There's blood on your shirt!'

'Nothing more than a scratch,' he dismissed her worry.

The soldiers gathered their guns and took control of the wagon. The lieutenant swore at the driver for being a part of the attempted hold-up. Renny informed him how the corporal had also killed a man in town.'

'That would be Sax,' Jess announced, drawing close enough to enter the conversation. 'He rode into Granville to warn you about the ambush.'

'You'll swing for this, Corporal Felding,' the Lieutenant informed him. 'Nineteen years in this man's army and you turn crooked.'

'Retirement due next year,' the corporal replied with a sneer. 'They don't pay much in compensation for the grade of corporal. I was to get a thousand dollars for the price of a bruise on my head.'

'Small pay when you consider you had to kill a man and these murdering scum killed Lockhart and Ponce.'

'It ain't my fault,' he whined. 'They promised there wouldn't be no killing. And there's no way I could live on a corporal's retirement pay.'

'You've lost your stripes a dozen times,' the lieutenant scolded him. 'You've no one to blame but yourself.' He turned to two of his men. 'Conner, you and Strode take charge of the corporal.'

'I could use a little help with a bandage, Marshal,' Lott spoke up.

'I know you, Lott,' Renny determined, recognizing the pair. 'And that would be your riding partner with a bullet in his leg, Ackers.'

'He's bleeding some,' Lott replied. 'We need to bandage the wound.'

'Yeah, hate for him to bleed to death before you both can hang.'

'Hey, we didn't do any shooting,' Ackers spoke up. 'Prince and Delaward killed the two troopers. Lott and me never kilt no one. We're robbers but we're not killers.'

Regina pulled Jess toward the man. 'He's a liar, Marshal! Those two men murdered my parents and my brother. They would have killed me too if not for the Hunkpapa Sioux arriving to scare them off. I was raised by the tribe, but I never forgot who killed my family. I saw your faces and heard your names.'

'Sure you want medical help?' Renny asked, displaying a smirk. 'Seems like a waste of time.'

The lieutenant ordered one of his men to get the medical kit. He was to tend to the wounded Felding and then Ackers. As for Jess, his slight injury was tended to by Regina.

Renny joined them about the time she had finished with the bandage. A wide smile was on his lips. 'I guess the mystery about how the gal here understands such good English has been solved. Did I hear right, she was raised by the Sioux?'

'Since she was nine years old,' Jess replied. 'I've got her some suitable clothes inside, but she pretended to be Indian while the bandits had control of the place.'

'Well, this turned out as sweet as drawing to an inside straight,' Renny said. 'And quite a haul for both of us, eh, Logan?'

'What do you mean?'

'Well, I'm willing to let you collect the bounty on Prince, but I sure earned a split of the reward for Lott and Ackers.' He scratched his chin thoughtfully. 'I believe I've seen a dodger on that other gent, Delaward, too. That's another bounty. Could be we'll both make a sizable amount of money for bringing those four in.'

'Why so generous about letting me have the

rewards for Prince and Delaward? Considering you kept the driver from shooting me, I would expect to share whatever bounty there is coming.'

Renny chuckled. 'OK, OK, I guess I'll have to be square with you. The army is also going to shell out a reward for us saving their payroll. In all, we're looking at something over a thousand dollars. I'm not greedy and you're right, I did save your life. How do you feel about an equal split of the reward?'

Jess smiled. 'Sounds fair to me, Marshal.'

'I'll want you to ride back to Granville with me. I need the help transporting the two bodies, the wounded Ackers and Lott. I imagine it will take a week or so to get our money for the bounties. If everything else is full up, you can have the jail cell.'

'We'll be glad to make the trip,' Jess replied. 'But we'll try the hotel first.'

'So what are you going to do with five hundred dollars?' Renny wanted to know.

Jess put his good arm around Regina and she slid in close to him. 'I think me and the missus will find a use for it.'

'Your missus?' Renny exclaimed. 'Well, that's sounds great for you both.'

'We only need a Justice of the Peace and I know you've got one in Granville.'

Regina looked at Jess. She had tears misting her eyes but there was no sorrow in her expression. 'You mean it? You would risk marrying me?' She shook her head. 'But you know I'm bad medicine!'

'Only to an Indian,' he replied. 'You're going to be goldurn good medicine for me . . . for as long as we both shall live.'

AUTHOR'S NOTE

For much of the country the winter of 1866–67 was the worst on record. Ranchers throughout the western states and territories call it 'The Big Die Off' because of the massive number of cattle and animals which were lost to freezing and starvation. Elsewhere, a four-day blizzard struck the Missouri valley in December 1866 dumping enough snow that it drifted over ravines and valleys two and three hundred feet deep. The treacherous storm condemned any man or beast trapped in the open to an icy, frozen grave, unless shelter was quickly found. Only complete fools would have ventured out into the deadly storm . . . unless they were men of compassion who would risk everything to save the lives of helpless women and children.

The rescue of Hunkpapa Indians during the horrific storm (described earlier in this book) is based on a factual account. The only addition was to include the story's main character (Jess Logan). All pertinent details of the rescue and immediate aftermath are included in the fictional retelling of the event.